Mim and the Klan
A Hoosier Quaker Farm Family's Story

Cynthia Stanley Russell

Guild Press of Indiana
Carmel, IN 46032

Library of Congress Number 99-65568

ISBN: 1-57860-036-7

This book is dedicated to Angela Stanley Russell

PREFACE

This book is a result of an urge that could not be denied. The characters had been stewing in my brain for years, and I delayed, waiting for them to gel further. One day, while I was musing about farm families who happened to produce only daughters, the Mim character, named for a friend of ours, leapt out and began to demand that I record her stories.

As I worked with Nancy Baxter of Guild Press, I learned more about the history of the Ku Klux Klan in Indiana and, gradually, Mim's story became linked in my mind with her location in Wabash County, next to Grant County where lynchings took place in Marion in 1930.

The era of the Ku Klux Klan in Indiana in the twenties is one of the most troubled in Indiana history. For most of the decade an organization based on intolerance dominated public thought and even government, electing mayors, representatives and the governor of the state. Young people need to know this dark side of our history, and more importantly, they need to know that Indiana eventually convicted the leader of the Klan, D. C. Stevenson, sent him to prison for a serious criminal act and rid itself of the Klan. We can be proud of our state's actions when we had to act against intolerance.

Much of the story told in this book is quite realistic. The Quakers in Indiana, like other denominations in our state, had members in the Ku Klux Klan, as well as flirting at times with its promulgated propaganda of temperance and Americanism. The stories of Mim and the cousins on the farm are based on the lives of my siblings, my cousins and me. The characters in this book, however, are fictional. The Wabash Meeting does exist and continues to be one of the most positively dynamic and fastest-growing meetings in the country. W.C. Mills existed, and he was honored by the city of Wabash when a school was named after him. Wabash was the first electrically-lighted city in the world. There was a Klan march in Wabash in the twenties and the Klan did march down the aisle of the Meetinghouse the next day. All the Klan history discovered by Mim for her term paper is a matter of record.

The Wabash Friends Meeting did not accept money from the Ku Klux Klan to build a meetinghouse, not in the twenties and not at any other time though other Indiana churches did accept funds from the Klan. There was no member of the church, to my knowledge, present at the 1930 lynchings in Marion. There is no evidence, to my knowledge, that the Klan fomented the Marion lynchings. While I have heard anecdotal evidence of the murder in Martinsville in the 1960s, there is no hard evidence it was done by the Klan. These are fictionalizations.

My great-grandmother was Clerk of the Monthly Meeting. On the other side, Grandfather Gurtner was Superintendent of the Sunday School. Other members of both sides of the family have served the Meeting. Many, many other families have been integral to the life and growth of the Meeting.

Acknowledgments

The author wishes to thank the veterianians she interviewed, the relatives whose stories she drew upon and the friends who served as volunteer readers.

Karen and Mim

Chapter One

"Mim, our history is part of who we are today. If we face it squarely, we can go on to better days." Grams Hanley

Cousin Karen and I were swinging our legs out the west door of the haymow, talking, while the late afternoon sun faded into a purplish sunset. I was hiding out from work. I'd been baling hay with the men all afternoon of this early September Saturday in 1969. My cousin and I couldn't have looked more different: Karen, with her straw-colored hair, was fifteen, a sophomore, short and slender. I was seventeen, beginning my senior year at the high school, not tall but mostly muscle after weekends and summers spent working for Dad, Grampa and Uncle Jesse on the farm. Hopefully young men my age could see past the muscles to the girl. I was pretty ordinary, with brown hair, but with auburn highlights. And I couldn't say I was partial to make-up. Sweat makes mascara run. You would have seen me dressed in the typical midwestern farmer get-up, blue-gray coveralls and boots.

We were talking about the new black Angus bull below us in his own specially constructed pen. "He's twelve feet long and more than 1,800 pounds," I told Karen. "Impressive, isn't he? If we can use him to father our dairy calves, the farm will save a bundle over time." It was exciting to have such a powerful animal in our barn.

"Dad says he could walk right through that gate, if he wanted to," Karen reported.

And that was true; bulls like this one just humored the humans who thoughtfully provided them food and cows for company. The big bull shifted his bulk below us, as we walked to the hole in the haymow floor where his hay was thrown down.

We bragged a little bit about our grandmother, Grams, mother of my father, James Hanley, and his brother Jesse, who was Karen's dad.

Grams and Grampa had a two-room apartment carved out of the first floor of the big white frame farmhouse there on the Old Farm, where Uncle Jesse, Aunt Maud, Karen and Thad also lived. Grams was Clerk of the Monthly Meeting of the Wabash Friends Meeting this year, her 75th.

"She does a wonderful job of keeping the Meeting focused without cutting off discussion too soon," I said. "And somehow her influence helps keep the grandstanders from taking off and dominating the group."

"Too bad every clerk can't have her skill. It isn't as if Quakers need to vote and Grams knows that," Karen said.

"No, Quakers work for consensus. The Clerk helps us avoid operating under majority rule, where the side with the most votes wins. Everybody speaks who feels led, and we work with a problem until all hearts are free of questions and we've reached a general agreement of what's the right thing to do. We've seen her do it."

My cousin was looking at the magnificent Angus. "I can't help thinking about the fair," Karen, a romantic at heart, sighed. She was talking about the Indiana State Fair, which we both participated in through our 4-H projects. It ended just three weeks ago. I came home with a State Fair blue ribbon, but no grand champion. This was Karen's first State Fair and she didn't win a blue, but we both were determined to return next year. Karen's specialties were strawberry preserves and a young man she met at the fair. Unfortunately, many boys her age didn't pay attention to girls yet. This particular one hadn't answered her letters. Karen's red-headed brother Thad, who was thirteen, had entered a hog this year at County Fair, and he certainly wasn't interested in girls yet, thank goodness.

"What I really want is a Quaker guy. Someone who already understands the way we think," Karen said thoughtfully. "Oh, well, how's Stalwart doing?"

Stalwart was my Holstein hope for Grand Champion at the next summer's State Fair in the cattle division. A year old now, he would be at his prime in another year. His breed was different from that of the bull over here on the Old Farm. The new bull was a coal-black Angus, while my Stalwart was a black and white Holstein. "Stalwart looks so good, Karen. How can he help it, though, with that champion blood in his veins? I'm so glad Dad let me leave him ungelded." Stalwart resided in the barn on the farm where Mom, Dad and I lived. Although he was my cattle entry for the 4-H competition for the next year, I had convinced Dad to leave him a bull for now.

Karen was genuinely interested, because she had a personal invest-ment in how well I did each year. At State Fair time, Grampa, Grams, Mom, Karen, Thad and I packed up and moved to Indianapolis for a week or so. That is, if one of us had an entry at State Fair. For an entire week, Mom and I didn't have to think about feeding calves or milking cows twice a day, no matter what.

Now Cousin Karen was off on how much she admired me for help-ing out on the farm. My dad didn't have any sons (or any other daugh-ters, for that matter). Traditionally, men and boys have done farm work, because it's heavy and dirty; the mechanical skills to fix machinery usually have been the province of men, and most times, men and boys are bigger than women and girls and have more muscle mass, a fact that makes a difference in a fight for leverage with a 1,600 pound cow or a 2,000 pound bull.

But in my case, I seemed to like nothing better than working with farm animals. I helped Grampa with the calves nearly every day: feed-ing, changing straw, watering. The dairy farmer needed the cow to freshen up immediately after the calf's birth (that is, give milk that can be sold), so the farmer took the calf away soon after birth, and substi-tuted reconstituted powdered milk for the cow's milk. Then for awhile, the calves were Grampa's and mine, even after they began to eat hay and grain in six weeks or so. They stayed nights in the feedway, a lean-to structure attached to the east side of the barn, closest to the house. They slept together for warmth, and we fed them milk twice a day in tin pails with big black rubber teats they sucked so hard they jerked the pail right out of your hand.

There were a lot of different skills in milking, like knowing how to sanitize every piece of equipment before you started. Knowing how to open the gate when you saw old Number 32 next outside the milk parlor door. If you opened the gate all the way, it startled her, she jumped and refused to come in. So you sorta slid it open about halfway. Number 32 would push it open the rest of the way and barge in, triumphant.

Some cows had to have their grain right away to get them to let down their milk, so you could get started milking. You might have a milker on their teats, but absolutely nothing would come out, until you gave them their ground corn. Others you had better hold off until later in the milking, or you had to feed 'em again to get the last of their milk.

Cousin Karen was talking again. "Mim, you look like a boy, swinging those bales. It's not like last year, when the bales were moving you around, which—come to think of it—was pretty funny!"

"I hadn't thought of it that way, over time. It certainly is easier for me to move them this year." I flexed my biceps tentatively. I'd been out baling hay with Dad, Grampa and Uncle Jesse most of the day. Dad paid me a dollar an hour, just to make it worth my time. With all the hours I fit in, even a dollar an hour added up. "Karen, you know, my muscles hurt, but a good hurt." What I didn't say out loud was that Mom wouldn't like how I looked—small pieces of hay sticking out of my hair and socks, torn sweatshirt, hay dust everywhere. Well, when did I promise to look good all the time?

"I don't get the same good feeling out of farm work that you do," Karen said regretfully. "I really could use the money. But my allergies! The hay fever from the field work would knock me out."

I agreed with her. "I couldn't work in a library like you do at school. I have to work outside."

"I know. Even for me, the thought of three years of law school after four years of college is sending me screaming!" Karen had told me but no one else she wanted to be a lawyer.

This Old Farm south of Wabash, Indiana, was Karen and Thad's home-place. Mom, Dad and I lived five miles east, on the other side of the north-south railroad track, the same track that Grams would tell Dad to be careful of every day as he left for home. I must have heard it a thousand times. "Be careful, dear, as you cross the track." This habit was easily explained, Karen and I surmised. It went back to an accident Grams and her father had at a railroad crossing in Marion in 1919, not long before she met Grampa at a Young Friends Conference at Earlham College. But I was getting "off track" again, wasn't I?

"Karen! Karen! Bring in the milk!" It was my Aunt Maud, Cousin Karen's mother, hollering for Karen to carry the milk up from the barn. A daily ritual for someone on the way from barn to house, a gallon of whole milk was carried up and refrigerated. We pasteurized, that is, heated to a temperature where most of the unfriendly bacteria died, but we didn't homogenize our own milk to stir in the cream, break down the fat, and evenly distribute it throughout. This meant we had a lovely thick layer of cream to skim off the top. If not for the excellent exercise in dairy farming, I thought all farmers would develop heart disease from the milkfat alone.

We climbed reluctantly down the haymow ladder. "I'm going to help them finish, Karen. You go ahead." Looking behind at me and still talking, Karen walked toward the farmhouse up the lane with the milk. Uncle Jesse had started late on the milking because of the long afternoon baling hay. With around seventy cows fresh at any given moment, the milking took about three hours, no matter when we started it. I lingered, hoping I could get Dad away to home a little early, because Mom would be waiting for us, with supper on the stove.

Out the open door of the cooling room next to the milk parlor, I watched the stars winking over the long, low toolshed to the south of the barn. This was where the tractors and wagons were sheltered from winter ice and snow. East of the shed was the farm gas pump. A farmer couldn't run into town every time he needed gas for the tractor.

The familiar sounds of milking drew me away from the evening sky into the milk parlor. Seeing what needed to be done from long habit, I opened the outer door of the parlor by its pulley for the next cow, then let her into the empty stanchion, the metal groaning softly as it moved. I washed her teats with antiseptic liquid, squirting milk from each quarter of the udder, plunking the milker heads on each of her teats. Then I pulled the lever to release ground corn into her feed bin. The rhythmic sound of the milker, alternating a pull and rest cycle, lulled cows and humans alike.

Grampa had already gone into the feedway to mix the calves' milk. "Mim, watch this for me, will you?" Dad asked. He was milking Bessy, who had a sore teat and needed constant attention. He went on out to the stall barn to see to bedding, and I stayed to help Uncle Jesse and watch Bessy. Dad knew I wanted to help with sick or injured animals, like the puppy with the broken leg that needed splinting long ago.

And the chicks that five year-old Mim helped feed cracked corn to every day. I grew fond of one in particular and tied a string around his leg so I would know which one he was again. Weeks passed and I forgot. One day I noticed a chick with a huge swollen leg, limping. I swooped and plucked him up and was trying to discover what the problem was, when horror of horrors, I realized my string had done this to him. I was extremely upset. In my little world, we did not hurt animals or cause them pain. We took care of them and made them better again.

When Daddy heard the story, he had me bring the victim to the kitchen table. With a starter bomb from the garage for anesthetic and a disinfected razor for a scalpel, we cut off the restricting string, then disinfected with methiolate. The chick recovered full use of the leg. This was Dad's finest hour in my childhood memory. Of course, the chick when grown had to go into the freezer with the others.

Bessy jumped and pulled off two of the suctioning milk heads. The milker began to gasp, and I moved smoothly in to put them back on, patting her on the side and talking as I moved. Milker must have hit the infected quarter and caused her to jump. I cranked her down another half ration of grain and leaned my head against her side, tired out.

"Go on up to the house, I'll finish." Uncle Jesse was being kind. There were still five cows out on the ramp to milk. He must have seen how tired I was. I took him up on it, heading for the house without delay.

Grams in the garden.

Chapter Two

As I passed the garden in the dark, I was surprised to see a flashlight and a shadow of Grams straightening up among the green beans. I walked taller, just seeing her. Grams always reminded me to stand up straight, especially as I wasn't tall, 5´3." Great Aunt Edith, Grampa's sister, was only 4´9," so the trend seemed to be upward. Grams called out, "Mim, can you carry this bushel of tomatoes for me? I'll get the beans."

"Sure, Grams. You want them in the back hall or by the sink?" I picked up the bushel basket and started up the path to the house ahead of her in the dim light, as her voice drifted up behind me.

"By the sink. Thought I'd pick while I waited supper for your Grampa."

"What did you cook, Grams?" I was hungry.

"Oh, hamburgers and a pot of stewed tomatoes with onion and green pepper sautéed in bacon fryings." This recipe was no surprise, as Grams' favorite foods were onion and tomato.

Walking past loaded shelves of colorful canned peaches and yellow tomatoes, I plunked down the basket for a minute, long enough to drag off my manure boots. Then I went on through Grams' pantry to her kitchen, and hoisted the tomato basket up by her sink, turning in time to help her lift her basket of green beans. There would be a lot of work between here and when these beans would be in jars in the back hall. Wash, snap the ends off, blanch in boiling water, then pack in hot, just-washed jars, filled halfway with hot water and a little salt, into the canner for so many minutes and out again, then watch closely to be sure the Ball jar lids popped down, indicating a good seal. If not, the beans had to be eaten soon or they would spoil.

I dropped myself into one of Grams' wooden chairs at the maple drop-leaf table in the far corner. Grampa and Grams' old farmhouse had better smells than ours. It was older, built in the 1880s, and older was better if it was good quality. Dad and Uncle Jesse grew up in this house, and now Uncle Jesse's family shared the house with Grams and Grampa.

Grams led the way on into Aunt Maud's kitchen. The old house had so many routes to the same place, a stranger could get confused. Aunt Maud was standing by the stove, stirring raspberry jam she'd been boiling down for awhile already. The raspberries were frozen in her big floor freezer last summer. Pint jars, lids at ready, were waiting on the counter. "Mom, help me pour, would you?" Grams washed her hands from the garden and put on hand-shaped hotpads. Boiling hot jam was vicious to bare skin.

I sat down with Cousin Karen, who was drinking her tea. Grams, finished helping, plopped her thin self down next to me at the big rectangular wooden table, and gave us a litany of what she had done in the garden today: three bushels of green beans and one of tomatoes picked and four rows of beans weeded. A minimum of an hour a day, as a habit.

We went back into Grams' kitchen, and as she was fixing me a cup of sassafras tea, the beautiful clear orange color filling the white china cup, she said, "Mim, you know we want to be sure you have a chance to be an ordinary girl. To dress up, make friends, date for heaven's sake."

This was a continuing conversation my Grams and I had. "I do know, Grams. But I keep feeling that you and Aunt Maud and Mom don't hear what I'm saying about belonging on the farm for good. Working with the animals feels right to me. I'll have all those things other girls have, but I wish you would stop trying to make me choose between the farm and the rest of the world."

Grams was watching me closely, a pleased expression on her face. "Before now, you were too young to know your own mind. Just don't forget there's a whole world out there . . . ."

"Mim, are you ready? Let's get moving. Good night, Mom." It was

Dad, coming in through the back hall into Grams' kitchen.

"Sure, Dad. Thanks, Grams." I was out the door into the back hall and into my boots and jacket in no time.

"Don't forget the railroad track, James!" cried Grams, as we whipped out the back door and hopped into Dad's truck waiting in the lane. With a wave to Aunt Maud and Cousin Karen in their kitchen window, we headed south down the road in seconds. We'd perfected a fast exit over the years. Otherwise, we sat back down and talked for hours, which could be great fun, but was hard on Mom, waiting dinner at home. It only took about seven minutes to cover the five miles home.

"I called Doc Tucker to check Bessy for mastitis tomorrow. And I want you to know what a good job you did on the hay wagon today," Dad said. "You're becoming more useful every year. The best part is you can blend in and help now. When you were younger, you had to be told what to do next, like Thad has to be. It's a maturing process."

"Thanks, Dad."

I thought about the day's work as we passed farm fields under the stars along the county road. After mowing with the haybine two days ago, Dad had flipped over the windrow yesterday to dry on the other side. Today we baled. I was responsible to keep the baler supplied with twine. When baling itself was finished, the men walked beside the wagon, throwing up the bales. Thad and I stacked them and then sat on top as Grampa drove the wagon in the lane from the field and up next to the south side of the big barn. Dad and Uncle Jesse went up into the haymow, while Thad, Grampa and I threw the bales onto the elevator. The elevator did the work of carrying the bales up to the haymow for Dad and Uncle Jesse to stack.

Thad helped where he could, but he was still trying to catch on to the various jobs. My freckle-faced cousin was only thirteen and his current fascination was planes, not farming. While my focus was on the animals, feeding and bedding, tending them, his eyes were on the sky. He made endless models from balsa wood and tape, throwing them from trees, haymows, off wagons. Still, I thought as we drove the bumpy road home, I really liked my Cousin Thad. He was a good kid.

Last spring, Thad and I helped with a difficult calving, one that led to the decision to buy the Angus bull. Dad had bred one of our best heifers, Rosebud, by artificial insemination. It was our last purely Holstein calf born. Holsteins had been getting bigger all the time, and that made for difficult births. This calf was too big for an easy birth, and, worse, was hung up in a breech position, meaning the back hooves were being born first, instead of the head. Uncle Jesse and Grampa were tied up in the milk parlor, so the three of us were out there in the dark. Thad held Rosebud's head. Dad and I had a rope tied to the calf's feet, and we were pulling, straining. The cow was pushing, her sides heaving. And groaning. After about ten minutes of this enormous effort, the calf was born. Dad pried open its mouth and wiped out the mucus, thumped on its chest, and yelled, "Breathe!" The little guy's eyes opened wide with fear and his chest started pumping air.

The calf born that night was Stalwart, my bull that would be entered in next year's 4-H cattle competition. We almost lost him. Dad said if he'd been stuck for another few minutes, he would have suffocated. Thad deserved his share of thanks for saving my Holstein's life.

I looked at the old house on the hill as Dad and I drove in our own barnyard: white frame farmhouse, two stories, standing lit, warm and waiting for us. We lived here because there wasn't room for us with Grams and Grampa and Uncle Jesse's all in the old farmhouse. And the men had decided years ago that their farm business needed more land anyway. I was glad we had our own place, though I spent most of my free time at the Old Farm.

Mom had a cheery supper ready: tomato soup, hot dogs and buns, chips, baked beans and lettuce salad with sliced tomatoes. The warmth in the kitchen made me sleepy. We told Mom about the baling and the new Angus bull's second day.

"He seemed restless at the end of milking," I said to Dad.

Dad counseled patience. "It's too soon to worry. He's not used to us or the place yet. He hasn't even been out of the pen, not until we're sure we can control him. It's no wonder he's impatient."

"Will he spend most days out in the pasture once he's settled? I hate to think of him just standing there, day after day."

"Oh, yes. He'll go to pasture in good weather and have plenty of cows and rabbits to watch."

"Tomorrow is Quarterly Meeting." Mom changed the subject, sneaking a look at me. I groaned inwardly. I had forgotten. Now I would miss watching the vet with Bessy because Quarterly Meeting lasted long. It was no use mentioning it.

"Maybe you'll see your friend from Amboy," Mom said hopefully. Mom harbored a wish that I would have a boyfriend soon.

"Sometimes I think you're going to enjoy my dating more than I do, Mother." She smiled, not at all put off. Mom liked to be kidded. She was talking about Nate, whom I met at last Quarterly Meeting at Amboy Friends in June. He was home from Purdue to visit his parents. Why hadn't I ever noticed him before? Well, the two churches only met together four times a year, not everyone made it to each one, and I hadn't noticed boys much until this year.

Anyhow, he was in his first year of veterinary school at Purdue. This meant he'd already finished an undergraduate degree, and had started in the School of Veterinary Medicine. Until the day that I met Nate, I had never thought about using my love for farm animals any way but as a farmer. We spent dinner time after last Quarterly Meeting talking about how he prepared for vet school and got into Purdue. We agreed that 4-H and Future Farmers of America were good clubs to belong to in high school, so the local farmers would know you down the road when you returned as a vet.

I agreed with Mom. I'd love to see him. "It will be great if he were there, Mom. I just don't want to get my hopes up too high. How often can a vet student give up a day of study? Besides I'm amazed you haven't said anything about the fact that he's four years older than I am." I headed down the hall toward the bathroom. I'd be asleep before my head hit the pillow, if I didn't get moving.

Mom's voice followed me toward the bathroom. "Your dad is four years older than I am."

On the way upstairs, after I showered and brushed my teeth, I considered how odd it was that I'd never thought about veterinary school before Nate. My attachment to the farm centered on the animals, working with them, caring for illnesses and injuries. It was probably because I didn't really enjoy school all that much. Academically, I was above average, but I did much better in subjects related to plants and animals. And a vet went to school seven or eight years past high school. Misery.

But always I knew I'd go to Purdue. Dad told me when I was in second grade I asked him, "And when I go off to college, where should I go?" And he answered, "Why, Purdue, of course."

Chapter Three

Dad was already over helping Uncle Jesse at the Old Farm with the milking when I crawled out the next morning. After a cup of coffee with Mom, I threw down hay and measured grain for Stalwart and the beef cattle we kept in the red barn on this smaller farm. I also checked the automatic waterer Dad and I installed a few years ago. He had mentioned it was running constantly, instead of only when it was empty. He was right—it was still running even though full. Probably the shut-off valve itself.

Now time for church, without Dad. He was too busy that morning. In Sunday School, I taught the six-year-olds this year. Today we were learning the story of the flood and Noah's Ark, with emphasis on God's promise to Noah. We colored, then cut out paper arks with various animal heads peaking over the edge, from the workbook.

Church was one of my favorite times, because I could relax, enjoy the singing and think about God's will, what that means for each of us. The Meetinghouse was fuller than usual. Folks from Amboy Friends were already here for Quarterly Meeting, when the joint business of the two churches of the Quarterly Meeting was conducted. First would be the meeting for worship, then the business meeting, then the potluck dinner downstairs. This day our minister, Zack Green, was guest pastoring another church, and we worshipped in silent meeting. We liked to honor Quaker traditions with an occasional unprogrammed meeting for worship.

The Quaker, or Friends Church, was founded in England by a man named George Fox about the time the Pilgrims came to America. Our religion had emphasized direct communication with God, and sometimes at our church services even today, we spend our worship time in silent waiting, until someone is led by God to share and speak.

Today I rested my mind for a moment, allowing my eyes to see the sanctuary I knew so well. A large, six-sided room with high, smooth, tan plaster walls, it was an unusual place. Up front, left of the pulpit platform, was the choir loft, unused for today's service. Above that were two balconies, built for even more choir members, now simply storage. Closing my eyes, I tried to focus on hearing the still, small voice of God.

Waiting for the Holy Spirit to move someone to speak can be unnerving. Sometimes no one speaks at all for a whole hour. If you listen for the urging of the Spirit, the pounding in your throat and dryness of mouth will tell you when you have to move out of your seat. At times you can be convicted to speak, but have no idea what you need to say until you're on your feet. Makes for exciting worship.

For some reason, God wouldn't leave me alone that day. And worse timing I couldn't have thought of myself. I hadn't spotted Nate yet. I was hoping he was here at the Meeting and I didn't want to make a fool of myself in front of him. But I was thinking about a joint Christmas program with Amboy Friends. I kept hoping this wasn't only about wanting to see Nate at Christmastime. Finally I got to my feet. "I'm feeling that I need to suggest a Christmas program for the whole Quarterly Meeting. Not just one church, not just kids or adults . . . all of us." And I sat down.

No one said anything about that for ten minutes. In the meantime, a few personal concerns from prayer lists were shared, and one young mother praised God for helping her learn more patience with her child.

Then Jerry Curtis, our choir director, stood and addressed the Meeting: "I've been thinking the same thing that Mim has spoken, that we need to draw closer together as a Quarterly Meeting. A Christmas program would be a wonderful way to start. I have a few ideas of what we could do, and I'm willing to organize, if you want me to. How about a quick meeting for all who are interested in the library right after the business meeting?" And he sat down. Silly though it sounds, a flood of joy ran through me, to think I hadn't dreamt it up out of whole cloth, just for myself. God had given him that idea, too.

After the worship time and the business meeting were over, I stopped by the library, then clomped down the side stairway with a couple of the kids from my Sunday School class on our way to Quarterly Meeting dinner. We came this way because the stairs were triangular, wrapping around in a tight spiral and they made play out of going down.

Downstairs, I saw Nate helping set up chairs with other young men from Amboy. Feeling suddenly shy, I headed for the kitchen to help set up the food, although it looked pretty much done. When I was coming out of the kitchen with the other women, he saw me and came over to claim my attention, so natural. He was tall, probably six foot, and not thin, maybe 180 pounds, with dark brown hair. We stood together for the prayer, then sat as though that was to be expected, and talked to each other constantly until nearly everyone was gone, and the remaining people were looking at us with amused smiles. One of his younger brothers came over, tapped Nate's shoulder, smiled at me, and led him away, with Nate calling over his shoulder, "See you soon."

Mom and Grams were in the church kitchen, finishing up dishes with the other women. Grams said in an aside to me, "What was his name again?"

"Nathan Daniels," I replied.

"For heaven's sake, I've known the Amboy Daniels since I was a girl at Marion Friends. His grandmother went to church camp with me. His granddad went to Purdue with your grampa. His mother was kind of sweet on your dad at one point, back in the thirties."

"Stop, Grams, you're overstimulating my brain with all of this," I pleaded. "He's just a friend I met exactly three months ago!"

"Surely, but from chance meetings, lifelong friendships are made," Grams said. Thank God no one overheard that one.

Well, except our friend Lucinda Lester. "Mim, Thomas and I met at church camp. Meeting someone within the church is a fine idea." She smiled at me and I fled, embarrassed.

When we stopped by the Old Farm for milk on the way home, Dad and Doc Tucker were in the stall barn with Bessy. "She has mastitis, Mim." While he applied salve to her front teat, Doc continued, "Oh, Mim, I met a lady vet at a conference at Purdue. She's working in a small animal practice in Warsaw."

"No kidding? Wish I could meet her."

"Well, wish no more. I've given her your name and here's her name and number. You're seventeen. You've got a license. Why don't you drive up after school one day and watch her in the surgery?"

"Oh, Dad, could I, please?" He smiled affirmation and we drove home.

Chapter Four

Monday I was in advanced chemistry with Mr. Barlow, who encouraged his female students in science. This was rare in 1969, when everyone still seemed to think science was for boys. I told Mr. Barlow about the awful conversation I had with my guidance counselor that morning. Mr. Richards, the counselor, told me he wouldn't register me for advanced science and math courses to prepare for the veterinary medicine program at Purdue.

"Bring in your mother or dad, Mim, and lay down the law to him," Mr. Barlow insisted. "If you let him keep you out of the courses you need, you'll be giving up any chance of vet school. No kidding. That's the end of it." I always knew Mr. Barlow was one of my favorites for a reason.

When Mom opened the farmhouse door for me that afternoon, the words of the story started tumbling out of my mouth. I was so angry, I couldn't wait for Dad. Mother listened gravely. While I thought that she didn't want me to be a vet, I guessed that didn't mean she would let somebody else tell me I couldn't.

"I'll be coming over to the school tomorrow morning, Mim. Where will you be at 9:30?" We made plans to meet by the principal's office during homeroom when I could get a pass.

I met Mom as planned by the front office. "Where is the counseling office, Mim?"

"Down here, Mom." The receptionist in guidance asked us if we had an appointment with Mr. Richards.

"No, but I think he'll want to see us," Mother said.

Oddly enough, Mr. Richards found time for us. "Now, Mrs. Hanley, what can I do for you today?"

"Mr. Richards, my daughter, who is eminently reliable in these things, tells me that you have refused to register her for the advanced math and science courses she needs in spring to be ready to apply for a pre-veterinary program at Purdue. Is this accurate?"

His mouth gaped open for much longer than he realized, I'm sure. We waited. Finally he answered, "Mrs. Hanley, your daughter could not compete with . . ."

"Mr. Richards, do Mim's grades qualify her to enter those courses that she has asked for?"

"Uh, yes."

"And has she taken the prerequisite courses to them?"

"Yes."

"If you do not now register her for those courses, I will today report this to your superintendent, the school board, and my private attorney. Do you understand?"

The man's face was gray. Needless to say, I was registered to the courses I needed.

The next Saturday, Dad and I were over at the Old Farm early enough for me to feed calves with Grampa, then eat gummy oatmeal with him. Grampa put a pot of oatmeal on the big oil heating stove in their living room when he left for the barn each morning, then it was hot and thick when he came back in. That morning, Grampa and I loaded on brown sugar, butter and milk to just the right consistency, and gobbled happily, leaning our cold feet against the hot stove. I got him to tell me about his courses at Purdue in 1918. He achieved his degree in agriculture, then returned to farm with Great Grampa. Wonder of wonders, he went upstairs into one of the closets and retrieved a few of his old texts for me to read!

"What was it like in this neck of the woods in 1919 when you got back, Grampa?" I really wanted to know.

"It was Klan country, Mim."

"The Klan—the Ku Klux Klan? In Indiana?"

"Yes, and inside our own Meetinghouse."

I knew what the Klan was from pictures in our social studies book. It was a group in the south which rode out at night years ago, wearing sheets and spooky hoods. The purpose was to annoy, intimidate and harass or even kill blacks and other "un-American people."

"Did you say here? At Wabash Friends Meeting?"

"Mim, when I left Purdue to come home to the farm, the Meeting had outgrown the original Meetinghouse. The Lester family donated land for the Meetinghouse, you know. The Klan was active in the Wabash community then, and I remember the Wabash klegel—that's what they called a local group—wanted to donate money toward the building of the new church. It was a hard time in the Monthly Meeting, deciding what to do. I don't remember whether we finally accepted the donation or not. Your grandmother and I were newly married and starting out here on the farm."

"But, Grampa, didn't people know what the Klan stood for? Cross-burning and hatred?"

"It wasn't so clear then, Mim, what they stood for, except we knew that the Klan was for Americanism and Prohibition and the Meeting was, too."

"Prohibition—a law to stop the sales of liquor in America."

"Yes, Friends knew of the terrible troubles alcoholism causes. I remember the church people and the Klan members would show up at the same public meetings in the early twenties, calling for a ban on liquor sales. Some of the folks from the two groups got friendly."

Grams had come back into the living room by then, from the kitchen where she'd been washing dishes. She stood listening to Grampa and then spoke: "Mim, my mother Todie Lenora was Clerk of the Monthly Meeting in the mid-twenties, after we had built the present church building."

Grams was Clerk now. I didn't know my great-grandmother had served, too. "No kidding?"

"Yes, and she would come home with a sick headache from Monthly Meetings when the Klan was trying to influence the church. I'll try to remember more."

"That would be interesting, Grams. I've always been fascinated by the Klan."

Later in the day, Grams set Cousin Karen and me to scraping corn off cobs into pans, using the jagged teeth of sharp saws. We had learned not to cut open our knuckles after a time or two. Cornroll was made with the corn pulp, plus egg, milk, salt and pepper. We baked it until it was golden brown, then added butter. Grams was freezing this batch for winter. Grams came in and out of the house, keeping us supplied with ears of corn and taking away full pans.

I told Karen what Grampa and Grams had told me. "The Klan was here in Indiana—not just the South. And it was here in our county—even among church members."

"I thought we were past all that bigotry—prejudice."

"Karen, I am ashamed to say this is a state that still harbors prejudice. Do you realize we have no black students at Southwood at all? Not one?"

"It's true, Cousin. I'm not sure there's a black family in this county."

I remembered a story one of the older guys on my bus had told me, before he got thrown off for fighting. "Did I tell you about the racist joke Bill told me on the bus last year?"

"No, and I'm glad you didn't."

"But, Cuz, think about it—the racist attitudes are still here. The story goes like this: Wabash and Marion flipped a coin for the Niggers and the hillbillies, and Wabash won. They got the hillbillies."

Karen knew what to expect from Bill, a rough kid from LaFontaine, but she was aghast. "No wonder you didn't repeat it. You know Paula who graduated last year? She told me that her brother doesn't want her to marry a black guy she met at her church in Marion, because he doesn't want his friends to think his sister is a 'nigger digger.'"

"Don't you hate that word? We're probably even more sensitive than others because Quakers in early times were persecuted, run out, and even killed for their faith."

Later I commented to Grams as Dad and I got ready to leave, "At least we know modern-day Quakers wouldn't be taken in by the Klan, right? The Klan may still be out there, but they don't touch us." Grams got an odd expression on her face, but it was gone before I had time to ask her why.

On the way home, I drove. Dad was thinking about me and vet school. He reminded me that besides admission, I had to think about studying hard all the way through, because qualifying tests for licensure must be passed at the end. "Dear, sometimes you freeze up on tests. Can you learn the material so well it won't matter?"

And a second cautionary note, "Are there too many vets? Is there room in the practice for new ones?" Dad had always been able to call my attention to things without offending me. These were real concerns I needed to research and consider.

After a visit to the Wabash library Monday after school (Mom let me drive), I researched and had the answer to these two questions. First, no, there were not too many vets. The demand, especially in small animal practice, was predicted to grow, not decline. Secondly, I could obtain copies of prior licensing exams to study. The current test questions would resemble the old ones. Repetitive exposure to the format and subject matter should help reduce my tendency to freeze up on standard tests.

While I was in the library, I also looked up the Ku Klux Klan in the *World Book Encyclopedia.* Seemed the Klan was founded by Confederate General Nathan Bedford Forrest, as emotions ran high in the South in the aftermath of the Civil War. The Klansmen, hiding behind sheets and hoods to disguise their identities, opposed the new rights for Negroes, using scare tactics like cross-burning and also actually attacking blacks. Membership was limited to white, American-born Protestants.

The Klan experienced a rebirth in the 1920s, led by Col. William J. Simmons of Atlanta, Georgia. Playing on the fears of job competition after World War I, the Klan sometimes used violence, threatening, beating and murdering blacks and their white sympathizers. Membership was said to have peaked nationally in 1924 at around three million. By the end of the decade, internal fighting, bad leadership and political opposition had hurt the Klan, and membership dwindled to a mere several thousand members nation-wide by 1929. When I stopped by the Old Farm to give Dad a ride home, I told Grams about my research and she listened carefully.

"Keep up the good work, Mim. I think you will be glad to know all you can about the Klan. Your Grampa and I will be thinking, too."

I didn't have time to tell Mom about the new Klan information that night. I had school work and wanted to get a day ahead, because Tuesday after school, I would travel to visit and interview Mrs. Elise Matthews, the veterinarian in small animal practice who knew Doc Tucker. Doc Matthews had been practicing for ten years in a storefront in downtown Warsaw, Indiana.

When I arrived, the receptionist took me back to the surgery and I watched while the doc opened up a dog's stomach to remove a nail he had swallowed.

"I knew I wanted small animal practice, because I grew up in town working with dogs, Mim," she told me. "My father was a general practice physician, my mom the town's only pharmacist. Our family bred English springer spaniels for show and sale and for pets. I spent every spare minute with the dogs, training, feeding, and treating their minor injuries. Vet school was the next step in a logical progression."

After the nail was out and the stomach sutured, I followed the vet on rounds, while she checked animals in recovery in the back cages. She answered questions: "Do you follow up with antibiotics after surgery, like humans?"

"No, Mim, most of the time it's not necessary. The animal population doesn't usually require antibiotics—they are still able to fight off most bacterial infections without aid."

"Why would that be, Doc?"

"Because resistance in the human population has been progressively weakened by antibiotic use."

She strongly encouraged me to persevere with my intention to attend Purdue in veterinary medicine and offered any assistance she could give in that pursuit, including loaning me her first semester books from school. I was in heaven. This summer I'd read them, if I could wait that long.

When I was a kid, I didn't play with dolls much. Hey! There was nothing wrong with dolls. But I had more fascinating playmates in the calves and kitties on both farms. I was out among the animals before I could walk. The photo album shows Baby Mim sitting on the grass with a Holstein calf above me, licking determinedly at my cap. I wasn't upset or afraid. When a newborn calf sucked on your hand, he pulled it all the way into his mouth, and you felt the roughness of the tongue and the hard gums as he sucked. As the calves got bigger, the sucking got too rough, especially as their lower teeth came in (cows don't have uppers, just a hard, bony plate to grind grain or grass against), and you had to walk around with your hands in your pockets when you weren't mixing milk for them in the feedway. I couldn't imagine a life without my cows.

But I also couldn't stop thinking about the Ku Klux Klan. When I got home, I updated Mom on my research and the conversations with Grams. "Right here in our county, they tried to drive out the Catholics and keep out black Americans. And influence our Meeting. Can you imagine?"

"Mim, why don't you do your senior term paper for social studies on the Klan in Indiana? You have yet to choose the topic. And we've been talking about a visit to the Statehouse and the State Library."

"Maybe I could spend a few hours in the Indiana State Library newspaper archives, researching the Klan in the twenties."

So it was settled.

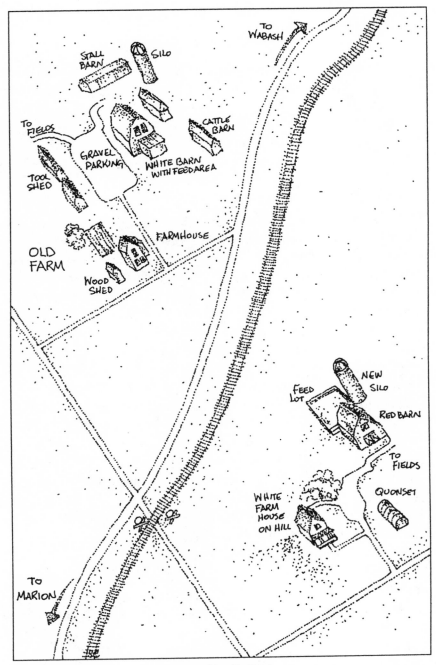

Map of both farms.

Chapter Five

W e had a scare on a Saturday in late September. Dad came up to the farmhouse at Grampa's, bleeding from a deep scratch he got when the new Angus bull shoved him hard into the rough-hewn boards of the pen. Dad was shaken up and more than a little irritated with himself for going into the pen with an animal he didn't know well. "Mim, you may be right, something may be making him jumpy. It's almost like he's not getting enough sleep."

Grams and I were scrubbing out the gouge, and applying methiolate to prevent infection. The shoulder and arm had already bruised pink and purple, where Dad absorbed the force up against the pen wall. "What could be causing such a reaction? Could he still be riled up by the move? Change of diet? Different straw in his pen? Could he be homesick?" His mind was moving a hundred miles an hour.

Dad and I went on home early to get a hot compress on his shoulder before it stiffened. Mom was smiling when she saw us coming in early, but she sobered quickly at the thought of nearly a ton of angry bull and Dad in the same pen. "You can't take a bull like that out to pasture, can you, Jim? How can you control him if he decides to be aggressive away from the barn?"

"You're right, Cecilia, you're right. Let me work this through. We've got to find out what's bothering him."

"Dad, it seems like the only way to know if he is being bothered at night is to watch."

"The longer I think about this, the more likely that seems to me, Mim. Do you want to be part of the night watch? Let me check with your Grampa and Uncle Jesse. Maybe we can divide up the night hours so each of us could take two hours and still get some sleep."

Mom wasn't happy. "Oh, Jim, she'll miss church." I held my breath. I wanted to help.

"Cece, I think helping solve the problem is more important than church just this once. We have more than $2,000 in the bull. He's supposed to father calves with the Holstein cows. We need a solid performance from him or the money's down the drain."

So I ended up taking a two hour shift from eleven that night to one in the morning. Any earlier and we figured one of us would have discovered the problem by now. It meant we'd have to spend the night at the Old Farm, but we couldn't think of any other way to know what was happening. Dad and I drove over in his dusty gold pickup. He lay down on Grams' couch and slept while I took the first watch.

Did I mention that Grampa kept a rifle in the house for varmints? Well, he brought it out to the barn that night. Loaded. He showed me how to hold it and fire it, though I could tell he wasn't thrilled to leave it in my hands.

"Mim, you must be very careful with this. It's loaded. Prop it away from you, where you won't knock it over in your sleep."

"Okay, Grampa, I'll be careful."

Dad would be back at one o'clock to take over the watch, and I would sleep for his two hours in the truck cab. He'd wake up Grampa at three o'clock and we'd go on home. Grampa would wake up Uncle Jesse at five, only an hour before Uncle Jesse rolled out for the milking anyway.

Pat had met us in the lane as we arrived. She was a black and white collie mix who was very fond of me, because she was a puppy when I was small and the only grandchild and we were great pals. Now she was old and I was only seventeen. Didn't seem quite fair. Pat was loyal to a fault. She would wait for hours by the door, if she thought I'd be coming back out of the milk parlor.

So I set myself up, me, Pat, the thermos of coffee and the loaded rifle, right on the ramp from the milk parlor between the bull pen and the feedway where the calves were bedded down. We washed and swept the ramp after every milking, so it wasn't too smelly. The calves were restless because of my presence outside their feedway at first, but they were tired and settled down soon.

Before I sat down, I hung over the side of the bull's pen, absorbing the fact that I was standing three feet from an animal twenty times my size. Stalwart, over at our smaller red barn, was almost as heavy, but he was rangier, less compact. And he was Holstein black and white, not the sinister black of the Angus. This Angus bull had muscles under his shiny coat so big, they defied description. His shoulders were almost as wide as I was tall. And I was trying to protect him? His pen was constructed of 6"x 6" timbers. But this was an effort to pen him in psychologically only. If he leaned all his weight on the pen, it would give way eventually.

My two hours were calm and boring. The bull's breathing indicated he was dozing next to me. Dad arrived with a new thermos of coffee at one o'clock, so I went out to the Ford truck and crawled under an old denim jacket on the front seat. Before I knew it, I was asleep, Dad was shaking my shoulder, and we were driving home. We passed Grampa in the lane, sleepily walking toward the barn.

Mom was thinking out loud the next morning. "Why did we have to buy another bull? We were doing fine with artificial insemination. Now my family is sleeping in barns, coming home before dawn."

We laughed and Dad said back, reminding her, "But, Cece, the pure Holstein calves were too big for the Holstein heifers to deliver, so we wanted an Angus bull to lower the weight and reduce problems at birth." He didn't intend to have any more Holstein bulls for breeding, although Holsteins produce better milk than Angus. Of course, I had already begun to hope secretly that Stalwart could fill that bill. How else could I keep my huge and growing friend?

When we came back in later from feeding the beef cattle, Dad checked with Grampa and Uncle Jesse. Nothing had happened on their shifts either. Not a thing. The bull snoozed away, not a care in the world.

The next day I had a postcard from Jerry Curtis, the music director at church, about rehearsals starting for the Christmas program. Mom and Dad both sang, but neither of them felt they should volunteer for this program because of other commitments. I was beginning to wish I hadn't said I'd help. It felt like I was behind in everything. I forgot to write that Dad and I were even later than we would have been the night before, because we hit a red fox on the gravel road on the way home. They were nocturnal, prowling around for small animals to munch on. We didn't like to kill them, even by mistake, but once done, Dad clipped the ears to take in to the county extension office where a small bounty was paid for killing them. All I saw was a flash of red in front of the headlights at 3:05 AM.

We had our first rehearsal for the Christmas program the next Tuesday. And we talked and came up with a plan I liked very much. The joint Christmas program would be Christmas songs, some sung by all of the volunteers, then a few solos, duets, small group renditions, a nice variety of songs and voices. With scented candles in the sanctuary and refreshments downstairs in a relaxed, informal atmosphere where we could come in and out, be part of the group or not, we would have a wonderful time and really experience Christmas together. This plan reduced the need for big, time-consuming practices. Jerry could schedule individually with the singers.

Then Wednesday morning, Grampa found Pat pretty well torn up by wild dogs, out by the silo in the empty feedlot. With a dog as beloved as Pat, even an old farmer like Grampa would call the vet. When I stopped by to help with the calves on my way home from school, Pat was lying asleep in their living room by the oil stove on a pile of old blankets. Her bites were all sewn up and bandaged.

Grampa told me what Doc Tucker had said. "She'll be fine with a few days rest, Mim. He's hoping she can heal without antibiotics and he'll be back to check in a few days."

"Grampa, at least Pat's told us why the bull is upset, right?"

"Right, Mim. No self-respecting bull could sleep while wild dogs pace around outside the feedway, just waiting to get at the newborn calves. It's the wild dogs, all right."

The bands of wild dogs were getting worse. Mean-looking, rangy characters, they lived in the woods out on the farms, running in packs, stealing lambs and calves, killing wild animals, and even raiding the alleys and garbage cans of the towns. Many of these animals were originally pets of city folk, abandoned out along country roads. Farmers tried to organize hunting parties to keep the problem down to a manageable size.

"Hey, cousin!" Karen was talking as we met on the lane on Saturday afternoon. As usual, she was carrying a *U.S. News & World Report* with her toward the barn. "I placed third today at the speech meet! All of my magazine reading is paying off!" Karen had joined the speech team in extemporaneous speech.

I turned around and headed back down the lane with her. "Fabulous! Isn't this only your second meet?" In extemp, the speaker was given a randomly-chosen topic of current news and thirty minutes with access to periodicals to prepare a five-minute speech. As we walked, I looked up at the huge weathered white barn and beyond it to the gray concrete silo standing tall.

"Yes, and I intend to do better next week! I'm headed to the haymow to read this." She gestured with the magazine. "What are you up to?" She read current events magazines constantly anyway, just from personal interest.

I was always surprised that Karen liked to sit in the haymow to read and talk. Thad complained that his sister wasn't any fun because she didn't like farm work. But Karen had been coming to the haymow since we were small, before he was born, despite the fact that her nose ran from her allergies. She loved the farm, especially the haymow, the one place in the barn where there weren't cows or men working or manure. We moved bales around to build tunnels and forts. One for each of us, if we wanted. The cats came in and out and could be coerced into playing. We could take food there because it didn't matter how messy we were. It was out of the rain. It was our place when we were kids.

"Oh, I'll go with you. I'm finished feeding calves with Grampa. Say, I'm driving to Indianapolis sometime soon to see the Statehouse and go to the Indiana State Library for my term paper," I said. "Do you want to go?"

"Absolutely. I need to get used to government buildings, if I'm going to be a lawyer. Count me in."

On Monday, the men decided the crops were ready for harvesting. Harvest time was special. From the moment the grain farmer determined the corn or soybeans were ready for harvest to the hour the last acre was cut, it was done in a great leap of intensity, as long as the weather held.

Weather being the major uncontrollable variable in the farmer's life, fathers and daughters or sons disappeared onto combine seats for the duration. Sometimes working far into the night if conditions were right, Dad and I hoped for unconditional support from the non-harvesting family member, Mom.

Mother carried food and drink to Dad in the fields during the hot days. I drove the combine after school. Mom's support role was very important: she never complained about our absence from normal activities. She listened endlessly to our stories of the last acre last night, the breakdown we repaired, or the moisture content and its impact on grain prices at the elevator.

And sometimes Mom wrote poetry about farmers and living out on the land. On the second Sunday morning in October, after a long Saturday on the combine, I found this by my plate when I struggled downstairs at six o'clock:

Farmer, Farmer

Farmer, farmer
Lover to the land
Till her, plant your seed
Bring bounty from your hand

Farmer, farmer
Go and find your wife
Tell her you love her
Keep her all your life

Farmer, farmer
Sons and daughters, too
Don't forget you must teach
Some to stay with you

Farmer, farmer
Softly comes the light
Rush of day, sunset fades
Stars and velvet night

Mom had surprising creative and nonconformist pieces to her. Why, when I was born, she stood against all resistance and named me Mim. People have asked me a hundred times what my name means, to the point where sometimes I told them it was an old Scottish name meaning a lively spirit. But the real story was, Mim was a family nickname for DeSylvia, Mother's favorite maiden aunt. They called her Mim. Mom named me Mim so she could hear it for the rest of her life.

Anyway, back to the story. It was hard to explain why we loved harvest time, except that was when the farmer could vary the grinding schedule of early and late milkings plus work all day in between. Instead, we were blessed with beautiful, starry evenings alone with the sound of the machinery and our thoughts. That year the weather was perfect and the yield high. Harvest was a time of celebration, not stress.

Chapter Six

That same Sunday, the second in October, was Monthly Meeting at our Friends Meeting. There was nothing too unusual about the Monthly Meeting process. Grams just called for the treasurer's report and committee reports, like Ministry and Council or the Christian Education committee which organized the Sunday School. Old business and new business were the two major categories that took most of the Meeting's time. Decisions, as I've said, were not made by a vote, but by a sense of the Meeting. Grams encouraged us to continue in prayer and discussion until we came to a group consensus that a certain path was the right one. "Are all hearts free?" she asked at the end. Deceptively simple. Keeping a community of individual believers focused on God's will instead of our own was not easy.

This Monthly Meeting was no exception. One of the little widow ladies had died, leaving proceeds from the sale of her home to the church. Several church members felt strongly that we needed to dedicate the money to the Building Fund.

Pastor Zack was open about his belief that we needed more space. "Our congregation is outgrowing the church. We need to start planning now for the growth God is bringing us. This building won't hold us much longer. And we'll need a Youth Minister soon. I can't keep up with the needs of our growing congregation without help."

Lawrence Jones, from one of the original families of the church, spoke up. "But what's wrong with adding on to this building? It was good enough for our fathers and grandfathers, why isn't it good enough for us? Why take on debt like that when the money could go to feed the hungry or support a mission?"

The upshot of the discussion was that Dad agreed to chair a committee to investigate the needs. One idea was to acquire property near the church where we would move the parking lot, then build another addition onto the east end of the existing church in the present parking lot. The problem with this was it didn't solve the most pressing issue: the sanctuary itself where we met to worship was too small and there was no room adjoining it to expand. We went to a two-service system last summer, and already both early and late services were crowded.

I drove Grams home, and she asked about my term paper on the Klan. "I'm going down to do research in the State Library in Indianapolis for it. Did you remember any more?"

"Mim, I think I remember the Klan trying to come into the Wabash Friends Meeting in the twenties."

"Really, Grams? What did they want?"

"Seems to me, and I need to talk to your Grampa about this to jog my memory, they wanted us to donate some of our offerings to the Klan."

A cold finger touched my neck. Another connection between the Klan and our Meeting. "In our very sanctuary? I never knew a thing about this until you and Grampa were telling me the other day. And I wanted to ask you—they're not here today surely? Aren't they mostly in the South now?"

"It's true, Mim, today they seem to move in small groups, mostly in the South. 'White supremacists', they call themselves and they aren't taken too seriously. But there are still active Klan groups here in Indiana."

"I know who the Klan victimizes now, Grams, but who was their target then? Not black people, like now?"

"In the twenties, they were against Catholics and Negroes. But there were no Negroes in Wabash, so the Catholics became the focus. I was so busy with my young family, I stayed back out of it, but I think they wanted to drive the Catholic families out of town."

"Why? That seems really odd today."

"Well, there was a lot less tolerance in those days. Some Protestants thought Catholics were trying to take over America. They had the idea the Pope was going to come over and rule here."

"But that's ridiculous."

"Of course it is. But a man named Al Smith was running for President and he was Catholic, and it seemed to make sense in a cockeyed way to folks."

"So they joined a group where they could hate Catholics together."

"No, it wasn't that obvious. It was a social activity to belong to the Klan in Indiana. There were picnics and rallies for America. We had just come out of World War I when everybody needed to be highly patriotic to weather the war together. And the Klan preached Americanism—put the flag on your window and so forth. And some people didn't see the dark side of the Klan because they didn't want to."

We had reached the Old Farm. That was all we had time for that day. It made me all the more determined to learn about the Klan in Indiana. Invading my beloved Meeting! I persuaded Mom to let Cousin Karen and me drive to Indianapolis the next Saturday, so I could research in the old newspaper files at the Indiana State Library.

Saturday morning, we were off early. Mom had called the State Library for me during the week and learned the Saturday hours, so I picked up Karen at seven AM. We drove south on Highway 15 to Marion where we picked up Highway 37, cruising south all the way to Fall Creek Parkway. The stately homes were lovely along Fall Creek. Dad had told us to follow the Parkway a block past the Marott Hotel at Meridian, and turn south on Capitol, so we did, then went all the way down to Ohio, where we turned right and parked at a meter on the street. The Statehouse with its bronze dome turned green was on our left and the State Library to the west across Senate. We went inside to the information desk, where I explained we needed to read old newspapers. The attendant sent us downstairs.

Newspapers were maintained on microfilms. We introduced ourselves and I asked Mr. Selch, director of the microfilm department, to see newspapers from the height of the Klan era in Indiana. He brought us microfilms from the *Indianapolis Times, The Fiery Cross,* the *Indianapolis Star* and the *Marion Chronicle Tribune.* "Mim, the *Times* and three reporters won a Pulitzer for their coverage of the Klan in this period. You may want to search fall 1930, too, because I believe there was a lynching in Marion. That's what the *Chronicle* microfilm is for." He showed us how to operate the viewer and the printer on down the aisle and then left us to read.

Karen was a very good student when she wanted to be. When I tired of reading, she would take over for awhile. What we found was far more than we expected, a sobering look at the Indiana that was. It showed that the Ku Klux Klan, which started in the South after the Civil War to keep the newly freed slaves "in their place," had come in to Indiana and organized klegels, local groups, all over the state. A man named D.C. Stephenson was the head man. He made money literally renting out sheets and other Klan club material, and encouraged Klan members to run for office in each county. Incredibly, the Klan soon gained political control over counties and eventually the state legislature.

These headlines and stories were from the Klan's own newspaper, *The Fiery Cross:*

December 8, 1922:
"KU KLUX ASKS FOR SCHOOL REFORM"
"Richmond Council is growing very rapidly, having a class of 25 last Saturday night. Go to it you Quakers, we are for you."

January 5, 1923:
"KLANSMEN MAKE FIRST APPEARANCE IN HOODS"
"FIRE DEPARTMENT EXTINGUISHES NEW YEAR FIERY CROSS"
"WHITE-ROBED KLAN VISITS CHURCH AT MARION ON SUNDAY"
"THE FAMOUS MUNCIE KLAN BAND"

January 21, 1923:
"FT. WAYNE KLANSMEN ACT AS GOOD SAMARITAN"
"FRANKLIN KLAN HAS UNSELFISH SPIRIT"

February 2, 1923:
"PORTLAND, INDIANA, MAYOR FAILS TO STOP PA-
RADE OF PATRIOTIC AMERICAN CITIZENS"
"KLAN HAS MEETING AT COLUMBIA CITY"

NOVEMBER 16, 1923:
"75,000 VIEW KLAN PARADE." The article claimed 8,000
Klansmen marched in this Fort Wayne rally.

NOVEMBER 7, 1924:
"MAJ. ED JACKSON ELECTED GOVERNOR BY A WIDE
MARGIN" over his Roman Catholic opponent.

The December 8, 1922 *Fiery Cross* was particularly interesting:
"WHITE SUPREMACY LEAGUE MEETS"— ". . . the league is
in need of some big, red-blooded all white gentlemen to serve on its
board, and anyone aspiring to such a splendid and much-needed movement, speak over our phone . . .. We already have lawyers, merchants,
court judges, governors, United States and state senators, and several
splendid, fearless white men who are members and have welcomed such
an opportunity—that of membership in the White Supremacy
League—to express themselves. Let us hear from others."

There were ads in *The Fiery Cross* for Klan-owned businesses in small
towns all over the state: Anderson, Greenwood, Kokomo, Plainfield,
Evansville, to name only a few. The *Times* stories made it very clear
that D.C. Stephenson, Grand Dragon of the Klan, and his henchmen
dominated the Governor's mansion, the Indiana legislature, the county
courthouses, the police, and, yes, even the churches in 1924-1926.

The Klan visited churches and accepted "gifts" of the offerings to
further the Klan's corrupt and murderous aims. The Knights of the Klan

purported to be in favor of one-hundred percent Americanism, while cheating, bribing and stealing elections across our state. Catholics and blacks were their favored targets.

Sometimes called "the invisible kingdom" and the "invisible empire," the Klan developed membership in all levels of government. Membership may have risen as high as one in three Protestant men in the state in 1926.

Finally D.C. Stephenson, now head of a corrupt system of Klan-elected officials who would keep all blacks and Catholics down, went too far. He got drunk and kidnapped a Statehouse employee he knew, Madge Oberholtzer, took her on a train to Chicago, forced her to have sex with him and wounded her. The wounds festered, sickening her, but Stephenson would not let her go. In despair, the young woman poisoned herself and eventually died. The newspaper articles recorded Stephenson's sensational trial in the Hamilton County courthouse in Noblesville, where a jury found Stephenson guilty of murder.

Karen and I were incredulous at this cesspool of Indiana history. "Look at this!"

"Can you believe it? Here, read this article." Mr. Selch had to come and ask us (nicely) to be quiet.

Finally (we'd had about as much reality as we could take that day), following the microfilm director's lead, we scrolled forward to 1930. There was more Indiana history to face: even though the power of the Klan was broken, a last terrible act had to be reviewed. On the front page of the August 8, 1930, *Star* was a photo of a limp figure hanging above the courthouse lawn in Marion, Indiana. The photo captured the crowd behind the victims. Expressions ranged from sadness to cheering.

The Indianapolis Times headlined, "STATE ACTS TO PUNISH MARION MOB, DOUBLE INQUIRY STARTED INTO LYNCHING OF TWO YOUNG NEGRO SLAYERS." A mob of 4,000 had gathered outside the Marion jail late on the night of August 7, 1930. About seventy-five men broke into the jail and dragged out two of three young black men accused of killing a white youth and attacking his sweetheart. They hung one outside the jail and the other from a tree on the courthouse lawn. Not fifteen miles from our homes.

I copied the article and the photo, and we left, sick to our stomachs.

"Mim, let's walk through the Statehouse to calm down." We entered through the north door, up the steps. The Statehouse is built of Indiana limestone. The first floor is beautiful and spacious, with mosaic tile floors and wood-paneled hallways. We walked around, past the offices of the Attorney General, the Secretary of State and the Governor, then took the elevator up to stroll by the Supreme Court offices and courtroom. After that, we rode down to the basement floor where we found the friendly clerk at the Blind Stand. We asked her where would be a good place to eat and she told us about the Canary Cottage on the Circle, so we went there for chicken salad and muffins, a real treat. All in all, a trip worth making.

Chapter Seven

The days were shortening dramatically. Halloween came and went. I couldn't believe how fast the year was going. I remembered the year previously in the fall when my Holstein bull was growing straight up, not out, with knees and ribs and searching tongue everywhere. He was enthroned as the king of the barn at our house, where he was the sole Holstein. In his little pen next to the Angus steers, he spent nights in the safety of the barn, then relished days in the fields with the steers. While they grazed, he soaked up the vanishing sunshine and galloped by their chubby bodies.

I switched him to corn and hay at about six weeks, as soon as he started showing interest. No more baby treatment with powdered milk. He was an important long-term project for me.

Another Saturday morning came, and Mother and I were out in the yard, planting bulbs. The last of the leaves drifted down over flower beds where chrysanthemums looked long and droopy. While we planted, I told her about the Youth Group hayride the night before. The Dell family, north and south branches, kindly sponsored hayrides every year as long as I could remember. Wagon, hay, tractor and hot cocoa and cookies to warm us up afterwards. All this and an extremely patient driver. We were a noisy bunch.

I had packed blankets and a thermos of coffee and then went over to collect my cousins. We were running late because Thad wasn't ready when I got there, of course. By the time we got to the party, everyone was pretty much already packed onto the wagon. I found my friend Rebecca and her boyfriend Dick in a front corner under a red wool blanket, and Karen and I settled in next to them, Karen sneezing from the hay. It was cold, but the stars were bright in a dark blue sky. I could hear Thad laughing with his friends in the back where it was bumpier. The whole wagon of us sang folk songs like "Michael, Row Your Boat Ashore" and "Puff, the Magic Dragon." I wished I had a boyfriend to take with me, too. I thought of Nate. You could hardly call him a boyfriend, could you? Anyhow, I told Mom all the details, right down to what kind of cookies. She liked this stuff.

She was looking at brown bags she'd filled at the seed store. Each had a scribble in black crayon. "What bulbs this year, Mom?"

"Oh, just more tulips. A few more bright spots for the yard." We planted a circle of tulips, yellow and red, around the telephone pole. Across the gravel drive was the gray metal shed where the toolshop was. We put a patch of blue hyacinth bulbs right in front of it. The tractors were parked inside here in the worst weather.

After bulb planting, Mom let me drive the car, a robin-egg-blue Ford Fairlane, on over to the Old Farm, where I found Grams dressed warmly in the chill wind, pulling up the last vegetables in the garden. Frost several nights had ended the garden growth. Soon everything would be rotting if not picked. Grams was particularly interested in the green tomatoes, from which she would make piccalilli, an east Indian relish. The rest would be laid out on newspapers in a window in the sun, not touching each other, where they would continue to ripen one by one, sometimes all the way to Christmas.

Picalilli
1 qt. chopped green tomatoes
2 medium-size sweet red peppers, chopped
2 medium-sized green peppers, chopped
2 large mild onions, chopped
one-half c. salt
3 c. vinegar
1 lb. or 2 c. firmly-packed brown sugar
1 tsp. mustard or 2 T. mixed pickling spices
Combine the chopped vegetables. Cover with the salt. Let stand

overnight. Drain and press in clean thin white cloth (pillow case or sheet) to remove as much liquid as possible. Add vinegar, sugar, and spices. Simmer until clear. Pack in clean, hot, sterile jars. Fill to the top. Seal tightly. Makes 3 pints.

Later the cousins and I in our jackets helped Grams pick up walnuts from the row of trees along the lane. Pat obligingly chased the squirrels away from our nuts. The fallen walnuts were left on the drive for a few weeks so the trucks and cars could help take the tough green hulls off. Then we gathered the nuts, knocking or hammering off the remaining hulls before placing them in a basket so they would begin to dry. Your hands and nails would turn absolutely green if you didn't wear gloves doing this. By Christmas, the nuts were ready to be cracked with a hammer, then shelled, a tedious task. No one was as patient about shelling as Grams. She could do any number of other things mentally while her hands went on shelling black walnuts. I tended to absent-mindedly eat the nuts I shelled, so that by the time Grams had a cup of walnuts, I had a quart of empty shells.

The milk truck pulled in on its twice weekly pickup. Tom, the driver for many years, handed butter packages out the window to Grams as he backed past us toward the barn, then maneuvered the rear of the big tanker close to the milk parlor door.

Thad and Pat followed him down and stood in the parlor doorway, watching the process. I'd seen this so many times. First, Tom opened the top of the bulk tank, making sure the automatic stirrer had been on, then he dipped for a sample clear down inside with a long dipper. Using a pre-packaged kit, he checked the sample for leukocytes or white blood cells. This was a check for mastitis in the herd. If the white blood cell count went too high, we'd be shut down. He also checked for particulate matter, a measure of cleanliness in the parlor.

Grams turned away from the scene to take the butter in to the refrigerator. Karen and I carried the walnuts in their bushel basket to set behind Grams' heating stove to dry. "Mim, next Saturday we'll do chickens if your mother can have us over at your house then."

"Okay, I'll check and let you know, Grams." I rarely went close enough at home to see how Mom's chickens were doing. It is difficult to explain how bad a lot of chickens all together smell. But Mother went loyally on producing the fryers and roasters for both farms for the freezer. This in addition to her own garden, the yard and the flowers, and she took care of the house with almost no help from her farmer daughter.

Anyhow, I checked with Mom and she thought next Saturday would be fine for freezing chickens at our house.

The next Saturday, the first in November, Grams and Grampa, Aunt Maud and cousins Karen and Thad arrived around eight o'clock from five miles down the road, and we assembled in the sideyard of our farmhouse, ready for work. Mom and Grams brought out the vats of boiling hot water. Thad went to the chicken coop, bringing two at a time. Grampa quickly snapped a chicken's neck, then chopped off the head on the block. After a quick dip for the unfortunate fowls into the vat of hot water, Karen and I plucked off the feathers, quite a lengthy process. Thad stopped by to tell us we weren't working fast enough. He could carry chickens to Grampa faster than we could pluck them.

In the house Mom and Grams gutted the chickens, hurrying them into the freezer in large plastic bags. Fifty chickens ready for winter, in three hours. Not bad. Later I scooped out the chicken coop with a shovel and washed it down with the hose. It wouldn't smell much better until the cold of winter. Loose feathers would blow around the yard for a day or so, providing fun for the kitties in the sun, batting the feathers with their paws.

That week I wrote out an outline for the Ku Klux Klan term paper and found what books I could from the Marion library. Together with the original newspapers Karen and I had copied, I just might have enough.

Chapter Eight

The Angus bull was leading a normal life. The wild dogs were evidently gone. My term paper was almost done and not due until the end of the semester, so all was right with the world, just in time for Indiana Yearly Meeting of Friends at Earlham College in Richmond in early November. In years past, Dad and Uncle Jesse had rotated Yearly Meetings off, so that one of them was home milking.

Grampa and Grams always went, and Mom and Aunt Maud. And of course, we three cousins. Over a lifetime, each Quaker developed her own network within the larger church. The rich network tied us together, encouraging us to bring more of our whole selves to the church community. Did I make the point strongly enough that these meetings were important in many ways? After all, Grams and Grampa met at a Young Friends conference, or we three cousins wouldn't be here, would we?

Anyhow, as long as I could remember, Uncle Jesse and Dad had never been able to get away at the same time. Dad and I were sitting at Aunt Maud's table, eating her colby cheese and saltines and talking. Aunt Maud said, "Jim, it's time we gave these kids a chance to prove they can manage without us, don't you think? After all, Mim milked all by herself again last week. With Thad helping, we might be able to get you and your brother to Richmond at the same time for a day or two."

And so it happened that Thad, Karen and I stood in the lane at the Old Farm on a late Friday afternoon, waving good-bye to the six adult Hanleys. A cold November wind and dark, angry sky made us realize we needed winter jackets and gloves.

Dad would be back Saturday night late, after the banquet. He planned to hitch a ride back with another Wabash church member. The others would drive back late Sunday after the Quaker Lecture. Thad and I looked at each other as the sound of the big Olds 98 dimmed to the south. Three milkings, just us. Karen wouldn't be any help.

"We can do it," I said. "I know we can." I didn't even mind not getting to Yearly Meeting this once.

First things first. I moved my overnight bag with toothbrush and Sunday clothes, in case we actually made it to church, into the east bedroom. The upstairs at the old house had a central hallway leading to four large bedrooms with tall windows. No matter what you did, the wooden stairs creaked when you went down to the bathroom in the night. I used to go, "bomp, bomp bomp" on my rear end down those stairs, playing.

Anyhow, Aunt Maud and Uncle Jesse's bedroom was the west one, with Thad in the north and Karen in the south. The east bedroom, which looked out over the front yard toward the road and the east woods, was the guest room. It had a four-poster bed left by one of the great grandparents who lived here when he got really old. Of course, Grams and Grampa slept downstairs in the bedroom-kitchen of their compact two-room apartment.

The cousins had followed me up. "Man, it's weird to be here without them," Thad muttered. "It's quiet."

Karen asked, "Do you think we should cook or start milking? Silly question! I'll cook, you two start milking!" Karen had this all figured out.

We swung our way around the banister at the top of the stairs, and clomped down, fast. "What's for supper, sis?" Thad was starving already and we hadn't milked one cow. Karen made him a quick sandwich of yesterday's roast beef out of the refrigerator.

Thad and I went toward the barn to start the process of hooking up the sterilized milker heads next to each stanchion. As we walked, my mind wandered back to prior Yearly Meetings. I had made several friends among the young people who came year after year. I'd have to write them and explain my absence.

The college environment in Richmond was memorable. The student center at Earlham had a graceful winding staircase. The new library, built in 1964, was open and airy, yet substantial. And then there was the Glass family tombstone in the Friends Cemetery, which many a coed had been invited to see. I could always imagine that conversation in my mind: "No, seriously, there's a Glass tombstone there. Come on, let's go see it."

On the last night of Yearly Meeting was the Quaker Lecture, a speech of some serious import, a commentary on Quaker doctrine, the state of the Quaker union, or any other topic that struck the speaker as timely and needed. The lectures had in the past been known to run three hours. Quaker scholar D. Elton Trueblood, Ph.D., had given several in the years I had been in attendance. The big challenge for us young Quakers was staying awake through the lecture.

As I returned from my reverie, heading into the chilly barn, the Angus bull was stamping his feet hard, and hitting the side of the pen with his shoulder. This was an impressive sound, as a ton hit mere wood. I hurried the cow on down the ramp toward the barnyard, and perched above him. "What the hay? What's the matter? Slow down, you're going to tear the side out of your pen." He was obviously agitated, tossing his head, wild-eyed. I stayed there and talked to him, gave him a little grain, and he calmed down some.

Until Pat started howling, somewhere out by the west woods. Thad appeared beside me, his eyes wide. "What's going on, Mim?"

I quickly pulled away from the pen, because Thad sounded so scared. "He'll be okay. We don't want to agitate him any more. Come on, Thad, we'll milk, he's used to those sounds. And you call Pat in, okay?" And so we got back to it.

After three uneventful hours (Thad pinched only one cow's teat and she kicked at him, but he was pretty fast and got back out of her way), we cleaned out the milk parlor, sweeping out the manure to the barnyard with our brooms, and put the milkers into the sterilizer. Then we went on into the feedway to give the little calvies their milk. None of them seemed sleepy yet, like they usually do. Out to the stall barn to feed hay, I noticed the cows were restless. I knew something wasn't right. I didn't say anything more to Thad about it, not yet. Pat had been following us around protectively. Now she began to growl deep back in her throat.

We headed to the house. Dad and I had fed at the other farm before we left, so that was already done. "I'm beat and starving," Thad admitted as we dragged ourselves to the kitchen door.

"Don't come in that door! Have a heart, go in through the back hall and get out of those clothes," Cousin Karen urged. Spoken like a true farm wife! Obediently, we stopped, turned and circled the west side of the house to the concrete porch at the back and came in through the back hall, leaving manure boots outside and taking Pat in with us.

Karen had corn roll in the oven and hamburgers already fried on the stovetop. Green beans were heating in a pan. Wonderful savory smells drifted around the kitchen.

Thad and I plopped ourselves down.

"Gee, sis, how come you didn't milk for awhile? I didn't know Mim and I'd have to do it all."

"Yes, you did. When have you ever once seen me milk a cow?" Thad shook his head. "Tomorrow I'll help with the calves, okay?"

After supper, I gestured Karen back into the kitchen while Thad turned on the TV in the living room. Pat was lying next to the kitchen door, growling. "Karen," I said, "it's happening again. I think the wild dogs are back. The bull is getting upset, and even the calves know something's wrong. I'm going out there for the night. Where's Grampa's rifle?"

"First of all, you aren't going out by yourself. Thad and I are coming. Second, I've got really bad news: nobody but Grampa and Dad knows where the rifle is."

I couldn't believe it. "But why? Why have a rifle for varmints on the farm, and nobody knows where it is?" We were still talking low at this point. Thad had the television turned up pretty loud.

"You know how rambunctious Thad was when he was younger. The best way to keep him from blowing his foot off was not to tell him.

And I didn't want to know."

"Great, just great. They leave us in charge, but with no defense. And if we call a neighbor or the county sheriff, we'll never hear the end of it. You know they'll say, 'Girls—scared.' Dad and Uncle Jesse will never leave us in charge again. I haven't seen one dog yet, but I know they're out there."

Pat chose this moment to raise the growl to a howl. I petted her old head. "You can't go out, Pat. Remember what happened last time. Karen, we've got to find that rifle. I'm not sure we can keep the bull in his pen much longer if we don't drive them off."

"We'd better get Thad in on it. He knows more about the house from helping Dad with repairs than I do."

"You tell Thad. I'm looking for the rifle. Now would it be in the house or the woodshed? House, right? Where it would stay dry and handy." Karen headed for Thad while I went toward Grams' apartment, talking to myself.

"Logically, the best place to keep something from Thad would be in their apartment." I began going through the closet up under the stairs that entered from Grams' kitchen and bedroom combination. I squeezed in behind the big cast iron bed to reach it. Old hat boxes, luggage, and scrapbooks. Grams' dried wild flowers in cachet sacks, bringing a nice fragrance, but nothing lethal here.

Thad and Karen were rummaging through the downstairs closets in their side of the house. I called out, "Don't forget we have to put this back the way it was before they get home." I went on into Grams' pantry, which connected the back hall and her kitchen. Loads of places to hide a rifle in here. I opened every door, looked behind all the jars, and climbed on a chair to see the top of every cupboard. Nothing.

"Are you finding anything?" I yelled to the cousins. No answer. Must be upstairs by now. Yes, I could hear one of them clomping around in the walk-in closet between Aunt Maud and Uncle Jesse's room and Thad's. Suddenly, I heard something go clunk in the wall behind the cupboard.

Going to the stairs, I called up to Thad, "Hey, did you drop some-

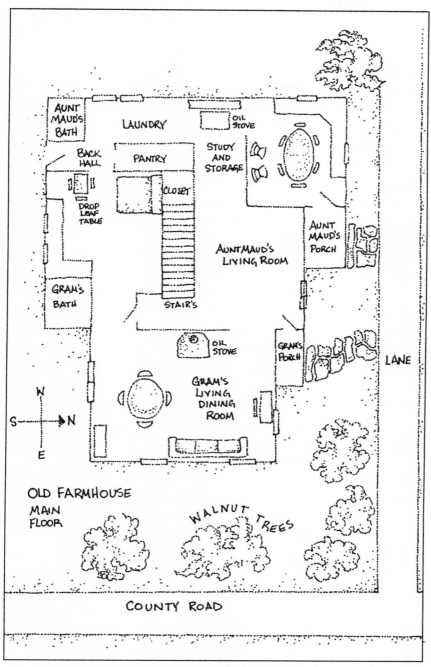

Diagram of the old farmhouse.

thing just now?"

"No, but I heard it, too. I was in the walk-in closet, looking behind Dad's stuff, when I heard a sound like something falling."

"That's it," I said, "that's what I heard. Come on down. Bring Karen." I showed them where I had heard the clunk in the cupboard in Grams' pantry. We tapped around a little on the cupboard wall. Seemed solid.

Karen looked thoughtful, like she was trying to remember something from long ago. "You know, it seems to me that Grams let something slip about when Great Grandfather, her father, lived here after Great Grandmother died. I guess he couldn't get up and down stairs very well, so Grampa built a dumbwaiter to carry food to him."

"Okay, that makes sense. They closed up the bottom end so we kids wouldn't find it, right? But if we heard something fall from upstairs, then that end must be open."

Pat was still howling in the kitchen. We rushed back upstairs with a flashlight. Thad started throwing things out of the walk-in closet like a madman. Karen and I looked at each other and shrugged. We'd clean it up later.

Flush to the wall of the west bedroom, there was a hinged section that had been painted over, probably twenty years ago. A very small latch kept it closed tight, almost indistinguishable from the rest of the wall in the dimly lit closet.

"Ah ha!" Thad twisted the latch, and it came open easily. Sure enough, there inside the wall was the dumbwaiter platform with pulley, a rifle and a box of shells sitting on it. "All these years, I was sleeping not ten feet from it and never knew it!" Thad lamented.

I grabbed the rifle and shells, and yelled "Stay here!" to Cousin Karen. With Pat on our heels, Thad and I burst out the front door of the farmhouse and made for the barn, where the Angus bull was bellowing and crashing around. We could hear that the wild dog pack had arrived. As we ran toward the barn, the dogs were lunging against the sliding feedway door, and it slid open. I could see the open door in the dim light from inside. The calves were bawling, the dogs snarling and snapping.

"Don't go in that way, Thad!"

"Mim, we're too late! They'll all be dead," Thad screamed back at me as we ran.

"Not if I can help it." I stopped in the lane and dropped a shell into the rifle in the moonlight, yelling at Thad all the while. Thank heaven Grampa had showed me how. "Thad, get back here. They might attack you. We'll go in through the milk parlor where there are doors we can control. You pull doors open ahead of me so I can shoot through, okay?"

He waited for me, his arms and legs shaking with excitement. We went in through the darkened cooling room to the parlor, switching lights on ahead of us. "We aren't trying to be heroes, right, Mim?"

"You got it, cousin." I positioned myself with the rifle up, at the door to the ramp by the bull's pen, and nodded to Thad to pull the rope to open it. I was ready to shoot when an incredible crash beyond the door made Thad jump back involuntarily. The bull bellowed so loud right beyond the door, I knew he really had smashed down the wall of his stall. A ton of bull on the loose. Hey, I felt sorry for the wild dogs.

The bull immediately pushed down the flimsy door to the feedway and lit into the dogs with his hooves. We could hear the fight but not see it. "Thad, we're out of our league with a loose bull. He's gonna kill every one of those dogs if they don't run away. Let's go shut 'em in." His eyes gleamed approval. We rushed back out through the tank room and around to the feedway door, grabbed it and slid it shut. It clicked into the latch. At least it would hold the dogs.

The bellows of the bull were deafening, even from out here, as he trampled those wild dogs to death. The concussions from the bull hitting the walls of the old barn as he maneuvered were frightening in themselves. Thad and I ran counter-clockwise around the barn, closing and latching the outer doors, hoping we could keep him penned in. I mean, hoping he would choose to stay inside the barn. All the while, Pat stayed with us, and we finally closed her in the outer cooling room so she wouldn't get in the middle of it.

I called the house on the cooling room phone, and told Karen to get on the phone and try to have Dad and Uncle Jesse back here as soon as

Black Angus bull with dogs.

possible. "Tell them we have a bullpen to rebuild. They'll get the general picture." In fifteen minutes, the awful sounds began to diminish and we peeked around corners, but always keeping close to the cooling room door to dart behind.

All in all, we lost three calves to the dogs' teeth and one to the bull's hooves and saved ten, but we found parts of eight or nine wild dogs. We weren't sure exactly how many. It was pretty messy in there. Like I told Grams and Mom, I was really very happy I didn't have to shoot that rifle. I was perfectly willing to turn the violence part of it over to the bull. He was better suited to it than I was.

Dad and Uncle Jesse drove in after midnight. They had decided we handled it just right, although the thing about the gun bothered them. Together we got a temporary pen constructed in time for a late morning milking. The dead dogs we buried in the back field, with Pat standing proudly on their graves.

Cousin Karen and I talked about this experience and the traditional Quaker avoidance of violence and weapons. Quakers were conscientious objectors in war! "Cousin, I see no conflict between our commitment not to use violence against persons versus protecting our farm animals from wild critters. Is a farmer supposed to stand around and let her animals be cut to shreds?"

"Mim, I don't have the answer. But I know killing isn't something I could do."

"Believe me, I understand. And that's surely what Dad felt about war." He had been a conscientious objector himself in World War II, because he could not possibly bring himself to take the life of another man.

I couldn't stand by and watch the calves die. There weren't any easy answers. There never had been. And if certain Quakers had supported the Ku Klux Klan in the twenties, the questions in front of the Meeting could not have been easy either.

Chapter Nine

Grampa and Grams had been working on more local material for my term paper, material I was not really happy to hear, but facts were facts, and history should not be rewritten, not even our own. They had been thinking and talking about that era, digging around in their personal files and remembering more.

I stopped by their house on my way home from school one afternoon in mid-November, when Mom let me drive to school. Grampa was sitting by the oil stove, leaning back in his wooden chair. "Mim, I talked to some other oldsters in the church, and we think that the money offered by the local klegel was accepted because a lot of church members were Klan members at that time."

My mouth dropped open. And I must have stared, because he went on. "Churches all over Indiana got involved in the Klan and Quakers were no exception. Some Quakers felt that the work the Klan was doing for Prohibition was so important it warranted their joining. And Klan members came to our church socials and church members went to theirs. There was a lot of singing 'God Bless America' and 'It's a Grand Old Flag' and children's games. As a group, the church was not yet aware of the hatred the Klan was promoting against Catholics and Negroes."

"I knew that was true in other churches, but I never realized the Quaker church was involved." I was really shaken by the news.

Grampa continued, "Money was accepted partly because of these overlapping memberships. The Clerk of the Meeting at the time, William Lester, was a Klan supporter and evidently some offering collections had been donated to the Klan. It wasn't until several years later, after the D.C. Stephenson trial in 1925, that the Klan members in the church were forced to confront the evil the Klan represented."

I knew who William was. He was Thomas Lester's father. Thomas, a friend of our family, had been Clerk several years before.

Grams had more. "By the time your great grandmother Todie Lenora was Clerk in 1925, the Klan was demanding that the church adopt the Klan's political agenda against the Catholics, the Negroes and the Jews."

"That must have been very hard for Great Grandma."

"There's more, Mim. I've asked folks in our Sunday School class to try to remember. You know Lucille—well, she witnessed a Klan march on a Saturday, must have been early in the twenties, we think. Klansmen four abreast, right down the Wabash Street hill from the courthouse, then west on Main. She was a small girl then and she watched them come in full white uniform, hoods and all, down the hill. She was up on the second floor of the National Bank where her father was doing business. The marchers turned west, past the pharmacy and then continued out of her sight. She says at least a hundred men."

I was devastated by events I had known nothing of.

"And the next day a group of Klansmen came into the Friends Church in their robes and hoods, right down the center aisle of the sanctuary."

"In our sanctuary?! But who let them in, Grams? Why did they come?"

"Well, first of all, no one had to let the Klan in—they pushed their way in where they were not wanted. But in our case, we think that William Lester was the reason they chose us."

"I can't see how anyone could forget that, Grams."

"This was early in the twenties, Mim. Almost fifty years have passed. All it took was some time to jog our memories. Your grampa and I were not in church that day. We had a new baby. So we don't have a memory of the event itself."

"Did the Klan continue to invade the church?"

"William Lester did little to lead the church away from them. Many people of the church were opposed to welcoming the Klan from the beginning. The internal struggle continued into Grandma Todie Lenora's days as Clerk. Finally the Meeting could not deny the cross burnings and the lynchings, and the Monthly Meeting decided to tell the Klan not to darken the church doors again."

"This is great material for my paper, but I'm not at all happy to hear it." I felt violated almost fifty years later.

"Mim, our history is part of who we are today. If we face it squarely, we can go on to better days."

"Grams, what did you think of the decision to search for land to build on?" Even with two Sunday morning services, there was standing room only, and the Monthly Meeting had commissioned Dad's committee to sell the old church, find property and build.

"The new church will give us room for a much larger sanctuary and more classroom spaces. We'll be out away from the old city streets, with no limit on how much parking we can build. I think it's time. As Todie Lenora said, 'Times change but challenges just keep coming.'"

Chapter Ten

Thad had begun doing more of the manure scraping, one of the most basic on-going jobs of the farm. The manure spreader, known as the honey wagon, was the second smelliest job, right after cleaning the chicken coop. The cows and the bull every day created a great opportunity to add naturally to the richness of our soil. Manure was scooped into the spreader with the little Ford tractor, then taken to the fields and spread, reducing the need for fertilizer. We all looked forward mightily to manure duty. It was year-round, never ending. Even Thad had begun to carry his share of this duty.

Now that there was ice on the puddles in the lane and the cows hurried out of the milk parlor across the feedlot to the stall barn after night milking, Mom and I started baking for Thanksgiving and Christmas. We had a certain number of new cookie recipes we wanted to try and cookie traditions to uphold as well. The deep freeze in the back hall allowed us to bake ahead and save confusion during the holiday season. Big tender sugar cookies. Chocolate chips so crunchy. Thick chunky peanut butter. Raisin oatmeal or butterscotch oatmeal. Black walnut applesauce (a personal favorite). Holidays brought visitors to the farm and visits meant cookies and coffee.

Black Walnut Applesauce Cookies

2 c. flour	1 c. raisins
half tsp. cloves	half c. shortening
half tsp. nutmeg	1 c. sugar
half tsp. cinnamon	1 tsp. soda

half tsp. salt   1 c. applesauce
1 c. nuts   1 egg, well beaten

Mix dry ingredients. Cream shortening and sugar. Add soda to applesauce. Add well beaten egg to applesauce, then to shortening, then to flour. Drop by teaspoonfuls on greased pan. Bake at 350° for 15 to 20 minutes. Makes 4 dozen cookies.

Despite the fact that I intended to have a career outside my home, I also loved to cook. 4-H and mother taught me to cook. From my first hot green bean salad with olive oil and vinegar to a full Thanksgiving dinner with yeast rolls and real mincemeat pie, I learned everything at the farmhouse. As the gardening and field work diminished that fall, Mom and I began to cook in earnest. Like squirrels readying for winter, we increased our stores of food as the chill deepened outside.

Casseroles had gone into the freezer for winter nights we didn't have time to cook. Vegetables were blanched, seasoned and frozen in supper-size quantities. Tomato-based sauces had been canned and were waiting on the shelf. Chickens were boiled and reduced for stock, which we canned in pint jars. Noodles were rolled out, dried and cut into strips, then frozen in batches. Sometimes I thought I'd like six children, so I'd have an excuse to cook for them constantly. Romantic idea. I knew the reality would be Cream of Wheat in my hair.

I was worrying out loud to Dad about this time that none of the boys at school asked me out. Without a brother, Dad was my primary source of information on boy-type questions. He said, "Intelligent girls frequently scare off high school boys. It takes a smart guy years to realize he needs a bright woman or he'll quickly grow bored."

"But that means I'll never date!"

"No, no," Dad laughed. "In college, smart women catch on with the men. Anyone you'd care about would want a girl who'd wear well for a lifetime." It was talks like these that reminded me why I was so fond of my dad.

Jerry wanted me to sing the alto in a duet of "Sweet Little Jesus Boy" at the Christmas celebration. My friend Rebecca from Youth Group would sing the soprano. (She and her boyfriend Dick had been on the hayride.) Rebecca was a senior this year at Wabash High School. Thad, Karen and I attended a different system, the consolidated schools that served the south part of the surrounding county. Anyhow, I talked to Rebecca most Sundays, although not so much when I began to teach Sunday School. Singing offered a great opportunity to catch up.

At church, Rebecca and I worked through the song seven or eight times. This particular song had sweet harmonies that deserved our very best. And Rebecca told me she was getting married in June and asked me to help with guest gifts at the wedding.

At November Monthly Meeting, Dad reported for the new church committee. "The northside Catholic Church is interested in buying our church building for a fellowship hall and youth center on the southside of Wabash. I think we need to wait for their offer and then give it serious consideration."

The church treasurer, our friend Thomas Lester, from that old church family that went all the way to the twenties, also sat on the committee. He stood up and said, "I am concerned, though, that we need to think about whether a Catholic youth center on the southside might draw our youth away from our own new church center." It was an odd, brief statement for Thomas who usually went on and on.

No one else had much to say on the subject.

Thomas, as he let me call him, was a particular friend of mine. He and his wife Lucinda lived several miles from the church, east along the Wabash River, on a farm with hogs. Thomas and Dad grew up together in the church, though Thomas was a little older. He and Lucinda were childless, and as I grew up, several times a year, I would go home with them after church, while Mom and Dad went to sing in nursing homes or jails with other choir members from the church. Thomas and Lucinda seemed to take to me. And I loved their hogs because they stank so badly and had tons of piglets that were fascinating to watch.

When Thomas served as Clerk of the Monthly Meeting, I was nine years old. He would let me stand beside him and hand out papers, and sometimes I had to wait a long time while he talked. Everyone said he was the most talkative person in the county. Lucinda was my Sunday School teacher when I was five. A very small woman, shorter than I was, she had a sweet way, lots of hugs, with tiny kids like no one else. I loved Thomas and Lucinda.

Our whole family spent Thanksgiving and Christmas together. Having no family of their own, Thomas and Lucinda came and ate with us. Thanksgiving was at our house this year. We were starving: one o'clock was later than we usually ate. Mom had been cooking alone today, because I had been out helping at the barn. Grams and Aunt Maud set table, while Karen carved the turkey on the counter. I stuck the rolls in their basket with linen napkin liner and put them next to the butter.

On the stove the turkey gravy rapidly thickened. The coffee was steaming. Cranberry salad, relish plate with pickles, chutneys, and fresh vegetables, the apple butter, and cream for the coffee all came out of the refrigerator to the table.

Mother finished the mashed potatoes, while Lucinda scraped out the gravy into the boat. Green beans with ham and sweet potato casserole with pecans were already on the table, and the mincemeat and pumpkin pies cooled on the sideboard.

The men and Thad were sitting around in the living room through the archway from the dining room, complaining cheerfully about the wait as we women worked. I slowed long enough to say to Thomas, "Do you really think a Catholic Youth Center on the southside would compete with us?"

He replied, "Well, better to be safe than sorry about it, you see, Mim." It didn't sound right to me, but we all had to go sit.

Finally at the table, Dad asked Thomas to lead us in prayer. "Dear Lord, today we thank Thee for all of the blessings Thou hast brought to our lives, especially the love of good friends. Please bless the work of Thy church here on earth. Help us to remember that we are Thy hands in the world. If something needs done, lead us to do it, Lord.

Thank Thee for the bounty of the harvest, and remind us of the stewardship we hold over the things of the Thy earth. Please bless our time together around this table. Move our hearts to contemplate the best in each of us on this day of celebration. We pray we may more fully serve Thee each and every day. Amen."

Karen, Thad and I sent grateful glances each other's way. A relatively short prayer for Thomas.

Chapter Eleven

"December Quarterly Meeting is after church on Sunday." Mom was just reminding me that Nate might be there, as though I would forget. Interesting to me that my memory of that whole day was telescoped into sitting next to him at dinner downstairs, when he asked me if I'd like to go out the next Friday night. "Of course," I said, nodding like an idiot.

"Where do you want to go?" he asked.

"Why not go into Wabash since you'll already have driven from Amboy?" I said.

"No, I'll be coming from Purdue."

"Oh. Well, why don't we just play it by ear that night? What time? Do you want to pick me up? Do you know how to get to the farm?"

"No, I don't—how's seven? Why don't you write me directions with the phone number?" Now you must understand, this was all being said in the midst of little kids and people our parents' and grandparents' age. It wasn't easy to get privacy in the middle of a church dinner.

And so he came. With the darkness already arriving before seven, he had a little trouble finding us the first time. I didn't know the road sign at our county road was down. After several false starts, he got the right road and pulled his blue Cutlass in about quarter after. We had to get through the curious parents, then we were finally out the door. "Back by midnight, Mom."

We talked nonstop all the way to Wabash, pulled into the A&W Root Beer stand and ate hot dogs, talking for two hours, and then were almost late for the last movie at the Eagles Theatre (it was "Airport"). We drove home in time to be in the lane at midnight, where we talked until one, when Dad flashed the porch light at me. I got the message, no problem.

Nate and I looked at each other, embarrassed for the first time, and he leaned over and pecked me on the cheek. We both laughed and smiled, and I raced out of the car, with him calling after me, "I'll call you as soon as I can."

It was the best night of my life. Dad asked what we did, and I told him all about it. Mom was a very good sleeper. She could sleep through anything, so I had to repeat the story at breakfast. Well, I left out the kiss in both stories, okay?

From that weekend on, Nate and I talked at least once a week and went out several times a month. With his studies, there was simply no way he could come every weekend. Mother and Dad promised I could go visit him at Purdue for a weekend in the spring, if we were still dating. I could live with that. For now, he had become my favorite person. How could I ever have been so lucky as to find another Quaker to feel this way about?

I finished my term paper on the Klan in Indiana. The D.C. Stephenson trial at the Noblesville courthouse and the breaking of the Klan's power across Indiana after his conviction figured large. That seemed important to me: that the people of Indiana had found the Klan's leader guilty of murder when they had to. The Klan had come to the state, the Klan had grown powerful, but Hoosiers finally woke up and kicked them out of power. I turned the paper in on the last day before vacation.

Dad was waiting for me in the parking lot in his dusty gold truck when I came out that afternoon, so I hopped in beside him. I could live without the school bus for one afternoon. "What's up, Dad?"

"The church attorney called, and he thought I should swing by to talk about a problem he's found in the title of the church. Thought you might want to go."

The church attorney's office was on the north side of the Wabash River. As we drove down the hill toward the river, crossing and starting up toward the rows of old brick buildings that form the downtown, I saw the courthouse high on the hill. Seeing it reminded me that

Wabash was the first electrically-lighted city in the world and the first bulb was installed in the courthouse. I guess it shone out over the city and caused quite a stir. Of course, this was long before my time. I read about it in the old newspapers in the Wabash library.

Frank Shambaugh was our church attorney. His building had been remodeled with lots of windows. Light streamed in on sunny days like that one. He welcomed us, then got straight to business.

"Jim, Mim, we've got a problem with the sale of the church. There's a cloud on the title, well, more than a cloud. William Lester, Thomas' grandfather, deeded the land at the corner of Pike and Vine to the Meeting in 1922. And the church was built there in 1923. However, the gift was not in what we call fee simple. The grant had a clause that said if the land or church building were ever sold to Catholics, Negroes, or Jews, the title would revert to his heirs. As it is written, you could not sell to the Catholic Church."

Dad could not believe what he was hearing. "Frank, I've never heard of such a thing. Is it legal?"

"I've never seen one in my lifetime. The conditional grant itself is not illegal. But the discriminatory condition in it is frowned on in the law and certainly would be struck by a court today."

"You mean we could have it changed?"

"Yes. However, you would have to go into court in a lawsuit, filing against the Lester family. The fight could be bloody and would tarnish the church in the public eye. A far better approach would be to get agreement with Lester's heirs informally."

"And that, of course, would be Thomas Lester. He's the last of the Lesters."

'Thomas will help out, don't you think, Dad?"

"I don't know, Mim."

Mr. Shambaugh went on. "Well, if Lester's heirs will sign a release, I will go to the court and ask for a change in the original grant of the church land."

I chimed in again. "Dad, maybe this is why Thomas didn't want to sell to the Catholics. Remember he spoke against it in Monthly Meeting."

"Maybe, Mim. Well, Frank, I'll talk to the committee and to Thomas. We'll see what we will see."

The joint Christmas program was held on the Sunday before Christmas, in the evening. After all my plotting to have him at the program, Nate had his last final the next day and had to study. The old sanctuary was lovely with candles lit in the windows. Rebecca and I sang "Sweet Little Jesus Boy" without a hitch. Other singers did "Silent Night, Holy Night" and "Away in a Manger." The whole group sang "What Child is This" and "It Came Upon a Midnight Clear." I watched Grams and Grampa's faces as they stood together, singing and holding hands. We had refreshments downstairs brought by the Youth Group, and they chose the wintergreen-scented candles for the tables. Folks were welcome to come in and out of the singing and talk and eat. Very informal, a work in progress, not a performance that came and was gone. It was a comfortable time.

Surprise, surprise, Mom and Dad and I met Nate's parents that night. The Daniels came up to Mom and Dad and made themselves known. Dad motioned for me to come over. "Honey, these are Nate's parents, Frank and Hilda."

Mrs. Daniels said to me, "Mim, your dad looks just like he did at Quaker Haven church camp." Mom and I smiled. We were proud of how young-looking Dad was. Nate's dad practiced veterinary medicine in Amboy, and Mrs. Daniels took care of Nate's three younger brothers at home. It was kind of a special night all around, even without Nate.

Christmas dinner for the Hanley clan was at the Old Farm this year. Aunt Maud was a good cook. The women and Pat were all in the kitchen when Cousin Karen started dropping the words "law school" into the odd conversation. At dinner, Grams commented that she surely hoped Thad wanted to stay on the farm, as it appeared more and more likely the granddaughters wouldn't be doing that.

Grampa had a wonderful surprise for us cousins: chests of drawers made by our special area woodworker W.C. Mills out of walnut from the east woods here at the Old Farm. "Oh, Grampa, thank you so much!

Where were you hiding these?" Karen and Thad were amazed at all of the plotting they hadn't noticed in their own house.

Despite the joyful distractions of the season, we were worried. Dad had shared the concerns about the church sale with Grams, Grampa and Uncle Jesse. He had already spoken to Thomas Lester informally, hoping for a simple answer, but Thomas had refused to agree to release the condition on the deed. The committee could not meet until January. In the meantime, the Catholic Church had given our Friends Meeting a written offer.

Wabash Friends Meeting might be in real trouble if the church could not be sold to the Catholic Church. First of all, even though Mr. Shambaugh said we would win if we fought Thomas' interest in court, to do so would be a negative, awful period in the church, Quaker against Quaker and friend against friend. Such a fight would be very personal and unwelcome to our family. Second, we had to sell in order to obtain a mortgage to build a new church. We might not find another buyer. Third, there would surely be a deep division between the Meeting and the Catholic Church, if we had to refuse to sell to them. And it would be impossible and maybe wrong to hide the fact that a Quaker, William Lester, had hated the Catholics.

Not least, I had a sneaking suspicion there was more to the connection between the Klan period in the church and that clause. Call it gut instinct. The timing was too close for there not to be.

The lane was a smooth plane of deep snow today, January 20th. No school bus came. I called the cousins as soon as I saw, and theirs looked the same. Goody, no school. I had my term paper back the week before and got an "A," so I was glad to take a mid-winter vacation.

I dressed and went out to feed my Holstein bull, Stalwart, who now dwarfed the steers. Dad had already thrown down hay and grain for the cattle. He was out on the tractor with the blade, clearing the lane.

When he was done with the lane, he yelled to me, "The road's only six inches deep or so. Maybe we'll try to get over to the old place."

"Sure thing." Grampa and Uncle Jesse would have to feed and milk alone at the dairy if we didn't make it, which would not be a catastrophe. They had milked without us many times before. But we'd get there if we could.

Mom packed us a lunch, while we put chains on the truck tires. The chains bit in the snow and gravel of the lane, catching and slipping. Dad was right. Once to the road, we moved along fine until we topped the rise to the south and found a long expanse to the stop sign at the corner that appeared much deeper. Dad got out and walked it. When he sank to his knees, he came back. "If this were an emergency and we had to get there, we'd take the tractor all the way. But it's not. We'll watch for the plows; maybe they'll come through by tomorrow."

Our county road was not a high priority for the snow plow. When we got back to the house, Dad called Uncle Jesse and Grampa, then went out to the toolshop to tinker with a small engine. I visited Stalwart to curry his coarse black and white coat. He had straw sticking every which way. I worked and worked with the brush. He was so big that his halter from last year wouldn't even fit over his forehead. "You haven't met Nate yet, Stalwart. He'll be here Friday. You have to be nice to him, because I think he might be the one," I whispered while I curried.

Stalwart loved this process and the attention. He would turn his huge head and just watch me with those beautiful brown eyes, while he chewed a mouthful of hay. I didn't like to think that he would be sold. "Oh, my, am I ever going to miss him when he's gone," I thought sadly.

But first he must go to the fairs—the County and then the State Fair—to be judged. He and I practiced setting him up for judging for a few minutes. The animal had to learn the stance so well that it became automatic. Then we went outside, so he could see and feel the deep white snow. The sun was out, and the air wasn't really cold. This was the first deep snow of the year, late for north central Indiana.

My presence started the other animals bawling for food. Stalwart bellowed back. I led him through the deep snow to the toolshop to show Dad how handsome he was. "Very nice-looking bull. And even-tempered. Too bad he's a Holstein. Have you showed him to Nate yet?"

"No, but he's coming next Friday night, if the roads open back up."

Chapter Twelve

We rallied around in the kitchen at noon, stomping feet and standing on the heat registers to thaw. Mom's bright yellow curtains and wallpaper really helped cheer up the wintry chill. She had made us tuna salad sandwiches and coffee to warm up.

"Cecelia, you and Mim will want to hear about the committee meeting on the church sale last night," Dad said. I sat down at the round wooden table, with my coffee warming my hands, listening. Maybe it would be good news, although I didn't think so.

"Okay, Jim, tell us everything." Mother didn't want Dad to carry all of this trouble by himself.

"We met from seven o'clock until late. First we offered Thomas a chance to tell us he would allow us to keep and sell the property—not try to enforce the 'give back' clause."

"Which is what the deed said?" Mom asked.

"Yes. He won't release it, and he wouldn't even give us a reason why."

"He wouldn't say why?"

"No, he's as tight about this with the committee as he was when I went to see him in December. When someone pushed him to explain, he got angry and said he would never go against his grandfather's wishes. That his grandfather had the right to not want his land used by Catholics or Negroes. He said if the church tries to sell the land to the Catholics, he will sue to enforce the condition subsequent and drag the church into court. And then he walked out. He didn't even seem like himself.

"After that, we talked about what we could do. Try to sell to someone else. Try to break the condition by challenging it. No one wants to do that. Then we tried to think how we could convince him he's doing the wrong thing. No decision was made. We prayed for an hour, and then went home."

There is something about a deep snow that makes people thoughtful, inward-turning. When Dad and I got to the Old Farm the next day, I stopped in at the house to deliver empty quart canning jars for storage in the back hall. I found Pat by the stove and Grams and Cousin Karen buried to their elbows in old photo albums. Pictures of Grams in her late teens, looking so much like Karen today it was uncanny. Grams' father was a banker, and Grams had twin sisters who died just after they were born. So she ended up an only child, just as I did.

Grams was a stickler for doing things right, and you could notice it especially in the winter when she could not be outside in the garden or working with her flowers. Last winter during the worst weather, Grams was sweeping her living room when I was over, waiting for Dad. She kept counting, "One, two, three . . ."

"Grams, what are you doing?"

She looked up from the sweeper. "Mim, I read that you have to cover a spot on the carpet seven times as you sweep to get it truly clean." Karen and I followed her around, fascinated.

The men were different. The animals had to be fed and the cows milked. Bad weather really didn't lead to the same symptoms of cabin fever. Uncle Jesse suffered with the gray skies though. He kept count of how many days of sunshine there were each year from winter solstice on December 21 through spring equinox on March 21.

While we were looking at photos, I remembered I wanted to show Grams something from the Klan research. I pulled out of my wallet the photo of the crowd and the still figure hanging above the Marion courthouse lawn. "August 1930, Grams. Lynching on the Marion courthouse lawn. Do you remember this?"

She peered at the copy. "Oh, yes, I do remember—my boys were very young then, and I was so busy, but I remember the newspaper story." Something caught her eye, and she leaned in closer. "Why, you know, I believe that's William Lester, there in the crowd, Thomas' grandfather who gave the land for the church. Oh, my heavens, that's Thomas, there beside him as a little boy."

Karen and I leaned in excitedly, peering. "Where, Grams? Which one?" She pointed to a man holding the hand of a small boy at the edge of the crowd. We three looked at each other and then back at the photo in disbelief.

"Why would they be there, thirty miles from home, the very morning after the lynching? There weren't any television news bulletins then," I said.

"Maybe they were in Marion to pick up feed or something?" Karen offered.

Grams told us slowly, "William Lester was one of the Klan supporters in the church. I didn't want to name names, because it's all forgiven and forgotten now. At least I'm done with it. But maybe he went on in Klan activities outside the church . . . Why would he be there in Marion the morning after the lynching? They lived north of Wabash then, just like now. It doesn't seem likely they would travel for feed all the way to Marion."

"What will we do, Grams?"

"We'll tell your grampa and your dad about it and see what they think."

When I got to the barn, I told Dad that we had something to show him in the house when he was done. Then I got busy. What they really needed was for me to take the Ford tractor and clear the snow for a wide path from the feedlot door of the barn back over to the stall barn. The cows were having trouble negotiating between the buildings. I fired up the little gray Ford with red fenders and scraped snow and cow manure out of the way for a path. While I was at it, I pushed the snow into two big piles in the corners of the feedlot. Next I helped Uncle Jesse and Dad milk for awhile, visited Grampa and the calves in the feedway, stopped at the bull pen to say hello, and carried milk up to the house.

While I waited for Dad to finish at the barn, Grams and I talked about all the generations who had served as Clerks of the Monthly

Meeting. Dad had done it, and Great Grandfather Ezra up Grampa's line, and Todie Lenora, Grams' mother. On my mother's side, Grandfather had been Superintendent of the Sunday School for many years. Perhaps someone before him was Clerk, we don't know.

"But, Mim, there are many other families in the church whose members have been just as active in leadership, if not more. That's one of the reasons Wabash Friends has survived and thrived. The Lester family, for example—William Lester donated the land for the church and he was Clerk of the Meeting before Grandma Todie in the 20s. And then Thomas served."

"Of course, Grams." In fact, I thought Thomas had done a good job, and he had let me help him, although he talked a lot for some Quakers' taste in a Clerk.

Dad clomped in Aunt Maud's door, shaking snow off his boots and unwinding scarves. "So what's up, Mother?" he asked, hanging his coat on the hooks behind the kitchen door.

"Mim and Karen have brought some information from the State Library that they didn't realize was crucial, Jim. Look at this." She spread out our photocopy and pointed to William Lester and Thomas at the edge of the crowd.

"For heaven's sake, it is him. I remember William from a little later, as I got older. No question it's him, Mim. And that surely is Thomas. So his grandfather took him to the Ku Klux Klan lynching. This may open a new line of inquiry and concern." He and Grams looked at each other.

Grams finished his thought. "As in, did William go on in the Klan, never mentioning it to the Meeting?"

I spoke up. "I have a horrible idea. Did his grandfather help kill the men? And did Thomas see it?"

By Wednesday morning, the snow plows had come through, so off to school we three had to go. We rode different school buses, as the farms were five miles apart. I saw Cousin Karen in the halls some days, and she told me stories about her speech meets. I needed the funny stories, after the disturbing possibilities raised by the *Star* photo.

Dad, Grams and I had had a difficult time deciding what to do. Finally we resolved to ask Thomas himself. Dad would call him and set a time to visit his home. Dad said this would be an old-fashioned eldering, my first. Quakers tried to follow the Biblical advice to go to a church member's home, when they were concerned that the member was taking a wrong path.

I hadn't seen Dad this unsure about how to proceed since he had to decide whether to vote for Richard M. Nixon for president in 1968. Nixon, a Quaker, had behaved in ways of which Dad didn't approve on the House Un-American Activities Committee, but loyalty to a Quaker politician finally won out.

The week began and I had to move on. I had to pick up forms for scholarships and an application for Purdue from the guidance office. I'd been dreading it. Seeing Mr. Richards again was not my idea of a good time.

Then an odd thing happened: I was asking the secretary in guidance for the application forms, when Mr. Richards rounded the corner. "Well, hello, Mim Hanley, how are you? Getting started on the Purdue applications? We're all going to be very proud when you're admitted to Purdue in pre-veterinary." Positively jovial, the man was. I thought about it later, and it seemed to me he had decided it was a good idea to support me. I was very glad. I could use all the support I could get.

I worked on the applications for hours that week. The financial aid forms were the most complex, requiring information from Mom and Dad's tax returns and mine. Some years I made just barely enough income on the farm to trigger a filing requirement. Anyhow, we got them completed, including an essay on why I wanted to attend Purdue, and I mailed them in. It would be months before I would hear.

I also spent time on this week's Sunday School lesson for the six-year-olds. The story was about how Cain smote Abel and killed him in the field. Cain thought he could hide his misdeeds from God. No, no. God knew what he had done and he made Cain a wanderer upon the face of the earth. But with six-year-olds we didn't emphasize the punishment as much as the right answer to Cain's question, "Am I my brother's keeper?" We colored pictures of brothers and sisters learning to live and play together without doing each other harm.

For me, the lessons of brotherly love meant a great deal. Mother lost a baby boy when I was very young. He never came home from the hospital. Mother couldn't have any more children after that. I didn't have a sibling by birth, so I had the great privilege of choosing my brothers and sisters out in the world.

We didn't have any more snow and made it to school the rest of the week. Snow was predicted for Saturday, but only a couple of inches. Nate came Friday night. At the last minute, I was saddled with girl-type cramps, so I was not enthused about going out. The four of us watched television together in the living room, Nate and I sitting together on the couch, Mom and Dad in their comfortable chairs. We ate popcorn and saw "Huntley & Brinkley" and "Star Trek," as the snow fell gently beyond the lace curtains on our long living room windows, the layers thickening without our knowing it.

About eleven Dad stuck his head out the kitchen door to check conditions, and yelled, "Nate, come here." When Nate got to the front door, he found nearly twelve inches of snow. The guys put on boots and slogged out to the drive to be sure the snow at the house wasn't just a drift, blown by the wind. Our kitchen door was on the northwest corner of the farmhouse, where it drifted deep.

From the dining room window where I was, I could see the two of them, standing talking in the snow, then Dad led Nate on out to the metal shed, probably to show him the engine he'd been working on. By the time they got back in, I was nearly asleep, and the decision had been made that Nate was sleeping over on the couch. Mom got him set up with a pair of Dad's pajamas, a pillow and blankets. I was tired enough, I just said goodnight and went on upstairs to bed.

In the morning, as I came downstairs, I could hear Nate and Mom talking at the kitchen table. He was telling her about his classes. I took that opportunity to take a leisurely warm bath. By the time I was through, Nate was out helping Dad with the morning feeding. Mom and I smiled at each other over our coffee. Fine with me. There was plenty of work for all of us. I went out an hour later and fed Stalwart.

Sunday was Monthly Meeting. Dad felt it was absolutely necessary for the entire Meeting to know about the church land problem, as the committee had not been able to resolve it, so that everyone affected could begin praying and seeking an answer. Dad calmly explained to the Meeting what the committee had learned from the attorney and that the offer to purchase from the Catholic Church had expired. Thomas and Lucinda Lester were not present in Meeting. In fact, Lucinda had stopped teaching Sunday School.

Grams had found a Minute from the 1922 Indiana Yearly Meeting on the Klan which she read to the Monthly Meeting: "It is important at this time for Friends to recognize that the Ku Klux Klan is a secret and oath-bound order. As a church we want to be fair in our utterance and relations toward all organizations, but we believe that the Ku Klux Klan by its hiding behind a mask is un-American; by its antagonism to a church is un-Christian; and by its fostering and fomenting race hatred is unpatriotic; therefore we would advise our members not to join it or in any way assist in its work." Afterward, she explained some of the history of the Klan and the Meeting that she and Grampa had gathered, as they helped me with the term paper. We felt, with the restriction in the deed, the Meeting needed to begin to know the context of that time.

Aunt Maud and Uncle Jesse were to drop Mother off, as Dad, Grams and I were due at the Lester farm after Meeting. We were armed only with the photocopy of *The Star* and our sense that something was seriously wrong in how the Lesters and the Klan appeared to be related. As we drove east along the road by the river, Dad talked to me about eldering.

"The idea is to bring your honest concerns into the room with the individuals involved, calling on God to illuminate the right path, Mim. We don't have to know what to do or say. We just try to follow His leading." I was still scared.

Thomas met us at the door and led us to their familiar sitting room, where I had spent so many happy hours. Lucinda looked like she had been crying. She didn't meet my eyes, just offered us coffee and left the room.

Thomas looked at Dad. Dad looked back. "You know what has brought us here, Thomas."

"Yes, but I don't know why you bothered, James. I have no intention of changing the restrictions on the church land my grandfather donated. I owe it to his memory to honor the family's wishes."

"I won't beat around the bush, Thomas. Mim, show him the photo." I did so, getting up, taking it from my wallet and handing it to him.

He looked at it, recognition spreading across his face. Tears welled up in his eyes. I thought he was going to tell us what he was feeling and thinking.

Instead, he walked over to the front door and opened it. "I'll thank you for leaving, James Hanley." He stood, resolute. A chill washed through me. Where had my friend Thomas gone?

Dad looked at Grams. And then at me. We walked quietly out the door. In the car, Grams said, "No one can help him until he's ready."

February was revival month. John Butterford, a minister from a Quaker congregation in Knightstown, came for a week of nightly meetings. We were pretty restrained folk normally. But during revivals there were altar calls and emotionally-moving songs ("The Old Rugged Cross," "I Surrender All," and so on). People you'd never heard speak in church stood up and testified or went down to the altar to pray. I sat with Karen in my favorite pew, a very short one at the back of the church, listening to the evangelist set up a rhythm in his speaking, drawing us all in.

Down at the railing, answering the altar call, were Thomas and Lucinda. They were there a long time. Nothing had changed about the sale of the church. The committee was at a standstill. But it was ever so apparent that God was working in Thomas' heart and mind. Dad said we needed to be patient to see what changes time and God would bring.

In March, on a happy note, my SAT results arrived. I did very well in math, scoring a 767 out of 800, which was 98th percentile. On verbal, I scored in the 90th percentile. We thought the scores would help me get into the pre-veterinary medicine program. Nate was certain I would be admitted. I didn't know—maybe yes, maybe no. My grade point average was 3.4, fairly mediocre for the pre-vet program. Purdue gets applications from a lot of 4.0s. The only thing to do was submit the SAT scores to Purdue and wait. Wait, wait, wait. That was what late winter on the farm always seemed like, waiting for spring.

Thomas and Lucinda had again been missing from Meeting since the revival. I missed them.

Chapter Thirteen

Finally in late April, spring break arrived. Nate spent two days of his with us. I took him out on the plow with me and otherwise put him on the same training regime I had used with Thad: learning to drive the tractor, mix calf milk, and wash udders. Believe me, this was plenty in a two-day period. Next time he could learn to open pulley doors in the milk parlor and maybe how to sterilize the milkers.

Grams and Karen were most excited at having him around. Grams plied him with cookies and unique teas to get him to talk about his family, many of whom she had known over the years. "Wasn't your Grandmother Daniels born a Jones? Was it Anna? Is she still living? We went to Quaker Haven together as children." And, "Your Granddad Daniels, he attended Purdue, didn't he?" Nate didn't seem to mind at all. He would go home loaded up with questions and greetings, and come back with a notepaper full of answers.

Karen was pretty shy about him at first. But soon she began to treat him like a brother. "Nate, would you bring me a cookie, too, on your way?" or "Nate, tell us how you managed not to break your leg when you slipped on the cow poop going down that ramp." A casual and familiar relationship. I enjoyed listening to it.

No, I'm wrong, Thad was most excited to have a young man around. He took Nate around with him, teaching him the most basic farm things, like not to pee on electric fences and not to grab the fence to determine whether it was on, even if your friend in rubber-soled tennis shoes assured you that it wasn't (somehow I don't think Nate needed this help). Thad spoke from experience about grabbing the fence. I wasn't there, but I guess the shock knocked him on his butt. Ouch, double ouch. Really painful.

Thad was milking now. Dad and Uncle Jesse could not resist organizing the four of us into milking squads of two each and competing against each other: Thad and Uncle Jesse versus Dad and me. The milk parlor began to resemble a time-study lab, with charts and diagrams of time and motion. Our times began to improve. At first we realized ways that seconds could be pared. After a few weeks, we began discussing a redesign of the milk parlor to radically improve time use. Winter boredom on the farm had set in. Dad had a pretty good idea for an octagonal milk parlor, where the farmer would be surrounded by the cows, the stanchions overlapping on the rear end of each. The only problem was, we'd have to teach the cows to back up better.

The lanes were full of muddy holes at this time of year. Tractors, pickup trucks and cars bounced and threw mud everywhere. Seemed to me it was time for a load of gravel, half to each farm. Mom's garden at our house drained earlier than Grams', and I could plow it now if I drove a tractor over. Mom could get a few early crops in, like carrots, green onions, and radishes. The men said it was okay to take the John Deere with the plow over on Saturday. I was glad for a chance to run between the farms, just to enjoy the good roads. Five miles at fifteen miles per hour took about half an hour, with crossing the highway and stop signs in between. Maybe I'd find a field or two to plow while the tractor was at our farm. The brown winter woods along my route were just showing a tinge of red and green, the colors of growing buds. It was going to be a beautiful spring.

Later, Nate arrived and we went back to the Old Farm to help Grams put her radish, lettuce and carrot seed in, plus cucumbers, squash, and a few gourds. Next planting day she would do peas, green beans, spinach, kale, corn, and sunflower seeds, and set in onion and tomato starts.

When we were finished, Nate and I drove over to home in his Cutlass and fed the beef cattle and Stalwart. That done, we each hopped into the shower and cleaned up so we could go to Marion and meet my friend Rebecca and Dick, her fiance, for supper and a movie. Their wedding was only two months away now.

"How long have you two been going together?" Nate asked Dick.

"Forever!" they laughed. "Since junior high," Dick explained. "We've never dated anyone else."

Later, on the drive home, Nate said, "Mim, I want you to date other people before you decide who you want to marry. I don't ever want you feeling you didn't have a chance to date anyone else."

I didn't say a word, because I already knew I wanted to marry him.

Chapter Fourteen

The first Saturday in May, the Youth Group made its annual trek to the W.C. Wells estate. Mr. Wells was the man who had made the chests of drawers for us cousins at Christmas. But W.C. was far more than a highly experienced carpenter. He was well known beyond local Quakerdom. Conversation at his table included the goings-on of the larger world of Quakerism: institutions of higher learning like Earlham or Friends University, the Yearly Meetings that Quarterly Meetings belonged to, and the overarching conferences like Friends United Meeting that Yearly Meetings affiliated with.

W.C.'s home was located halfway up the south bank of the river that runs through Wabash. The house itself, some fifteen rooms, was built into the hillside above an expansive pasture surrounded by hundred-year-old oaks and sycamores. A long gravel drive wandered past the lower meadow and up the hill to the house. On the east end of the meadow, hidden in a thick glen, was a free-running spring, its water sweet and pure.

Mr. Wells' basement workshop walked out onto the pasture level. There he worked with many varieties of wood. Physically, W.C. was a bear, tall and husky with a red face and the proverbial shock of white hair. He always had a smile on his face, which meant the twinkle in his eye was never lonely, Dad said. He built table games and lawn ornaments, rockers, cradles, bookshelves and birdhouses, and invented useful things, like the mailbox that could be unhooked from the post at the top of the hill by the person at the lever at the bottom. It slid down a chain, you emptied it, then pulled it back to the top by a pulley to where it clicked into place on the post again.

When we arrived, the Youth Group ranged through the house first, pausing for an hour to play board games at the huge dining room table. The north wall of the dining room was entirely windows, looking out over the meadow. Then into the living room to hear stories from W.C. and listen to music on old 78s. We quiet types stopped in the hall library to borrow classics from the shelves. It was there that I met Elsie Dinsmore and Jane Eyre years ago. Cousin Karen had read many more than I—nearly the entire wall. Next we gathered in W.C.'s workshop to watch him carve a bird. Then we burst out into the meadow, galloping over to the spring for a drink from the tin cup. We finally landed on the logs around the campfire. An hour of song and hot dogs later, we were pooped and meandered homeward. It was the same every year.

While I collapsed on the log, Thad and a friend were out in the meadow throwing a Frisbee. Thad loved airborne things so much, I knew he was studying the way the wind affected the wing. Pastor Zack reminded us to register for Quaker Haven church camp, which was a great place on Dewart Lake in northern Indiana, with cabins, a chapel and a dining room. Baseball diamonds, basketball courts, volleyball nets, fishing, swimming, boating and plenty of opportunities for learning about the living world were the order of the day at Quaker Haven. At camp, Thad and his friends were in constant motion, just like here, measuring things, observing them and then throwing them out of trees or off the pier to see them float. Even Mom and Dad went to camp there back when they were kids at Wabash Friends Meeting.

W.C. told us a story around the campfire: "My grandfather lived here when Indiana was forming a regiment of soldiers to go south to the Civil War. One night in 1863, the regiment gathered here in this meadow. They all drank from Grandpappy's spring and camped by their fires. In the morning, they started walking to meet up with Grant's army. Grandpappy often said he wondered which of them came back and which didn't."

"W.C., what did Quakers do during the Civil War? Did we just watch? Wasn't that a war worth fighting in?" Thad could be so surprising sometimes.

"Thad, those are good questions. Many Quaker Meetings sent bandages or donated money for the wounded on both sides. Some Quakers actually traveled to the battlefields to help tend the dying and the wounded. I remember a tintype of the Quaker poet Walt Whitman in one of the Army hospitals, comforting the soldiers. But some Quakers from the area went to the war. They felt it was necessary to fight for abolition of slavery, a great evil, even though Quakers are peaceable people.

"You could read their letters to friends back home in what's called the Green Collection at the Indiana Historical Society. But most Quakers did not go to war. They were conscientious objectors."

"Like my uncle Jim," Thad offered.

"Exactly right, Thad."

I thought about the Civil War, the men who left this very place on foot, and the Quakers who had to choose, as the fire died down to embers.

The next Saturday Nate had to study. At the farm, last summer's calves had to be dehorned and gelded (their male parts cut off) and neither process was one we liked. There was lots of blood and it was painful for the calf and the farmer whose instep gets mashed. This was not my favorite part of farming. Farmers called bulls who had been gelded steers; they were more gentle than bulls. This was what I had saved Stalwart from, the spring before, despite the fact that entries in the 4-H Cattle Division typically were steers, not bulls.

Later that day, Dad filled up the planter with seed corn and headed out to the field. I carried him a lunch and water around five, and he was still out there when I went to bed. We usually beat Grampa and Uncle Jesse to the field by a week or so, because the fields on this east farm drained better.

But both farms were planting by Monday while I was in school. It started raining on Tuesday, and was too wet on Wednesday. They got back in the fields Thursday and ran nearly round the clock through

Friday. By Friday night, the beans and corn were entirely in and I didn't get to plant an acre. I had taken a lot of food to the field, and carried seed corn and beans out to the planters in the truck numerous times after I got home from school on the days they planted. And Tad and I got to do most of the evening milking and feeding.

Anyhow, Saturday morning I stayed up in my room, resting later than usual and then straightening up. My normally mildly messy room had gotten entirely out of hand during planting. Work and school clothes were hanging from every door handle and chair. I made stacks of shirts and jeans that could be machine washed versus school skirts and blouses that had to be hand washed and pressed. I put away shoes in the closet. Clean socks Mother had washed for me went into the dresser drawer.

Once straight, the place looked not half bad. I had a very pretty natural wood bed and dresser set that Grandmother and Grandfather Gurtner had given me, with a pink and blue quilt on top.

Right then Mother was coming back up the lane from the mailbox. When she hollered for me, I looked out my north window, down to where she was coming toward the kitchen door. "Mim, it's from Purdue," she called. I headed for the stairs.

I was down those stairs and into the kitchen in, oh, maybe ten seconds flat, reaching for the envelope. Large, bulky envelope, return-address Purdue University. Then the fear hit.

"Mom, I'll be back as soon as I can open this." By the time I turned around and stepped into the dining room, I couldn't resist. I tore it open and it said dormitory assignment. Further in, I saw pre-veterinary listed as my tentative major. The wait was over. They had admitted me.

Mom was reading the same things over my shoulder. She hugged me without a word. I called Nate first. He was really glad. Guess he did want me closer! I could hear him telling his roomie, Terry, in the background. I was sure I'd meet Terry when I went to register for classes and pay fees. Oh, my, I told myself, now I'd have to deal with student loans, tuition and dorm deposits.

Before I let Nate go, I asked, "What's your lightest day this week?

I'm going to try to arrange a campus visit to check on financial aid and figure out my classes for fall at Guidance."

"Friday I could spend the afternoon and evening with you. Would the morning be enough time to do the paperwork?"

When I got off the phone I realized I didn't know how to find the two offices or how to get from Guidance to wherever Nate would be. I called Nate again. He was so excited that I was coming, he insisted on finding me a place to sleep so I could stay over to Saturday morning.

"Mom, I want to go over to the home farm and tell Dad and everybody in person."

"Of course, go. I'll cook something wonderful for our supper." I stopped by the barn on the way out and told Stalwart. And sang joyful songs on the way over. At the other farm, everyone was outside doing something. Aunt Maud, Grams, and Pat were in the garden. I planted a row of tomato starts with them and told the news.

"Oh, Mim!" said Grams fondly.

I hunted down Dad, who was with Grampa in the feedway, moving the calves that were weaned from powdered milk over to the stall barn. They were very pleased. After all, they both went to Purdue.

Then I went to the haymow, where Karen and Thad were talking. What a nice change, to find the two of them having a conversation, instead of arguing. At the news, the cousins immediately began planning to visit me often on campus in the fall.

Friday finally came and I buzzed out the drive in good time, with my suitcase on the back seat. For someone born in the city, West Lafayette and Purdue would not have seemed overstimulating. But I usually drove on roads where I met other cars only every few minutes. Reacting to the constant flow of traffic and pedestrians was exhausting. Even after I found the parking garage, getting into it was intense, with the tight spiral of cars impatient behind me. Thank heaven I had parked all those wagons at the farm. I reached the top floor and slumped against the steering wheel for a few seconds. Maybe this farm girl could not adjust to city life.

I went to Guidance and got a pre-vet class schedule tentatively planned. Registration wouldn't be until fall. Nate had told me it took place in one incredible day in the fieldhouse in early September. Within a few hours, 90% of the students would have their schedules.

Nate was waiting for me at the east door of Administration as we planned. He was dressed in slacks and a windbreaker. Early May weather is unpredictable in Indiana. He gave me a hug, then took me around campus with my hand in his or his arm around my shoulder. We grabbed Cokes to carry and swung by the School of Veterinary Medicine, south of State Street, which divided campus north and south. He identified his classrooms and showed me his locker for lab coat and books.

After that we went to the parking garage and moved Mom and Dad's car over by the off-campus house where he had found me a place to stay. Absolutely no one was home, but the front door of the big brick house was unlocked. Ash trays full of cigarette butts were everywhere, and even what Nate said were roaches, the ends of marijuana cigarettes. Smelled peculiar. Karen would have had an allergy attack in here. It looked as though four or five women lived there. We dropped my suitcase off and a note for his vet school friend Maggie that we'd be back later.

He took me by McCutcheon Hall to meet his roomie Terry, but he was gone, so we just walked and talked the afternoon away. One point on the tour was the Service Center, a tiny mall where we played at trying on rings in the jewelry store. At that point I asked him to the Junior-Senior prom.

"Tuxes or suits?"

"Suits."

"Yes, I'd love to." The man had the same resistance to dressing up that I did.

The next morning I was beat. The sounds of the city had kept me awake the night before. Mom wanted me in before dark, and Nate had piles of reading to do for Monday. I was amazed he had been able to give me an entire day of his company. So I headed home early.

On the way home, I thought about how peaceful my farm home was. I knew it would take me a long time to get used to the people and traffic at Purdue. And I'd had my own room all my life. What would it be like, sharing a dorm room?

Chapter Fifteen

The last Friday night in May, I was watching the evening news out of Indianapolis. The announcer reported that the Ku Klux Klan had obtained a permit to march through downtown Marion the next day. I called Cousin Karen.

"Karen, there's a Klan march in Marion tomorrow. I want to go watch. Are you in?"

"Yes, I want to go, but I think we'd better take reinforcements. Let's not be silly about this."

Karen asked Aunt Maud and Uncle Jesse, while I talked Mom into it. "We need to go see, Mom. Isn't it surprising that the Klan is still around at all? I would have thought all the criticism it has received would have put it six feet under."

"I think it is but a ghost of its former self, Mim." She agreed to go, if Dad would. He came in from the barn about then, and he said we could all go as a group and observe. As a learning experience. Grams and Grampa wanted to see it, too.

We agreed to rally the next morning on the east side of the Marion courthouse square, all nine of us, with folding lawn chairs and picnic hampers. But when we arrived, several hundred other people were already on the courthouse square. We had to go three blocks out just to find a parking place.

"Jim, I don't think we need to take the chairs. There isn't going to be any room to set them up," Mom said. I grabbed one chair, though, so I could climb up to see. We left everything else and walked back to the square, searching for several minutes until we had gathered our whole group.

There were several television crews, their trucks parked right on the grass of the square. The crews all seemed to be eating fast food sandwiches and laughing. The crowd was racially mixed. Businessmen in suits, women with kids, factory workers, young men and women, black and white.

And they were getting along with each other fine. Felt kind of like a Sunday picnic, except it was too crowded. A little kid ran into Grams, and as Grampa steadied her, he said, "Maybe we shouldn't have come. This is more than we bargained for."

"Dad, where were the lynchings, can we see the place from here?" I asked.

"See that big old oak tree on the south lawn, Mim?" He pointed south of the courthouse. "That's where at least one of them was hung."

The mood of the crowd around us changed. There was a stir up at the northeast corner of the square. "Can you see, Dad?" I yelled, because I couldn't see anything over the crowd in that direction. I climbed up on to my folding chair. Thad pushed his way up beside me, unsteadily. "Cuz!" I held on to him to keep from falling, as we teetered on the unstable chair.

Dad could see over the heads. He shouted to us, "Yes, there are maybe ten men in hoods and white sheets. The signs say, 'Nigger, go home' and 'Get the U.S. out of the United Nations'."

The crowd up in that area began to boo and yell things like, "Cracker, go home." The news people on the coverage that night called them hecklers. The marchers proceeded around the square. Several of the young black men from the crowd were running out close to the marchers, nearly touching them, then falling back, baiting them. Finally, one got too close and a Klansman swung his sign at him, bashing him on the head. When that happened, other men from the crowd rushed out and began to scuffle with the Klansmen, pushing and punching.

The crowd around us was surging, unsure what to do. The women of my family had their hands on us kids by then, pulling us away from the fighting. Uncle Jesse had turned red in the face, and Dad had to get him by the sleeve. We half ran toward the south lawn of the courthouse.

And then I saw Thomas Lester, standing alone by the old oak tree. It wasn't so crowded there, back from the ruckus on the north side. He had the strangest look on his face. I jerked on Mom's arm and pointed, and she let me go to him.

He didn't see me as I approached, being wrapped up inside with his thoughts. "How are things at the farm, Thomas?" He turned toward my voice in confusion. "Any big litters of pigs this spring?"

"Mim! What are you doing here?" He looked dazed by the reality of the place and the event, but he reached out to touch my arm, just like the old days, though his eyes shifted back to the oak tree.

I touched his arm and looked into his familiar face. "We came to see what the Klan is like today, Thomas. This is where the lynching was in 1930, right?"

"Yes, this is the place, Mim," he said, slowly coming back into focus.

"You were very little then, weren't you?"

Thomas looked down at me. Something in his face looked like it was opening up. "Yes, Mim, I was small. Grampa Lester brought me with him that night. We left home after dark and we met other men in robes here at the courthouse square. I was only six. The crowd was big, much bigger than this. And angry, yelling, screaming about hangings. I was afraid." He began to leak tears.

"I can imagine."

"Grampa took me back to the truck and told me to stay. As the night went on, thousands of people gathered. I climbed on top of his Model T truck to watch. Grampa told me years later that the Klan decided to wait for the crowd to grow to cover their actions. The crowd did it for them. The people were outside the jail, yelling and pushing, and then they broke down the door. They dragged the black boys out and hung one right over by the jail." He pointed northeast across the crowd, toward the brick jail around the corner. I knew where it was.

"Then they dragged the other one over the courthouse lawn and hung him from this very oak tree." He looked up at the tree again, his tears running down his cheeks.

Klan gathering in Marion.

"Did your Grampa help?"

"Yes, he had his white robes in the truck and he put them on when we arrived. From my place on top of the truck, I saw him help put the noose on the neck of the one by the courthouse, and I saw him pull up the rope. Afterwards, he hid his robes under the truck seat. Anyone could have found them, but no one was looking."

"And have you been in the Klan all these years?"

"Yes. It's not something I'm proud of, Mim. This has all brought that night back—horrible and so wrong. But I felt I should be in the Klan for my grandfather. He left me everything I own." He looked even more miserable again. "Mim, you can't tell anyone about this."

I hesitated. Could I keep this knowledge to myself? Should I? "I won't, Thomas. But I know you will do the right thing." He groaned and turned away. I turned and went back to Mom and Dad.

On the way home, Dad kept shooting questioning looks my way. I shook my head. "You taught me to keep a confidence, Dad."

"And I know you will, Mim. Thomas must deal with this himself."

May Monthly Meeting came around before I knew it. I knew Thomas was going to have to face the Meeting. No one could do it for him. But I was so busy thinking about all the changes that were coming on me, I lost track of when Monthly Meeting would be. After all, in four months, an entire planting season would be over, State Fair would have come and gone, and I would have started at Purdue. Big changes.

So I woke up, sitting in Meeting, when Thomas was getting to his feet, interrupting the business meeting and speaking to us all. It was a shock to my system.

"Mim, come and stand with me, will you?" He scared me, he was so pale. I got up from my pew and walked up and stood tentatively beside him. He reached out and took my hand. I looked at Mom and Dad for encouragement. They nodded at me.

"I need to get clear with the Meeting. I can't stand for this to go on. So many years and so much guilt." He stopped, his eyes filling with tears. Grams sat down on the front pew.

"What is it, Thomas?" she asked gently. "What does the Meeting need to know?"

"I've been a Klan member since I was a boy, Martha. The old Klan then and the new Klan now. I've hated Catholics and Negroes and Jews. I've hid this from you all, and I can't go on like this any more." His voice trembled. Gone was the eloquent Thomas we were all accustomed to.

Deep silence spread across the sanctuary. No twitching or paper rustling. Children quieted, as parents focused their hearts to hear. "My grandfather helped lynch a black boy on the Marion courthouse lawn one night in August of 1930. And I was there." The words came out slowly, and we listened.

"The men screamed and struggled for life. It was horrible. The sheriff made a weak effort to resist the crowd, but there were thousands of them, pushing and yelling, breaking down the door, and pulling the Negroes out. They didn't get a trial. I saw Grampa help tie the noose and hang them.

"My father was a Klansman, too, and I was always with him at the meetings. Even when I wanted to leave, I didn't know how. It seemed they were everywhere and they knew me and my family. You have no idea what that does to your soul.

"You may not realize it, but the Klan still exists. The tactics have changed some, but the goals are the same. It's a small remnant of the original, but the influence is evil. You may have heard about the Negro saleswoman who was warned to get out of Martinsville by dark and wound up dead in an alley . . . maybe you didn't hear, but I did."

His voice trailed off. He sat down on the front seat, exhausted. Grams got up and led us in prayer and the Monthly Meeting disbanded. Dad and Grams and Zack gathered around him, praying.

Chapter Sixteen

The weeks went by and gradually things unwound. Thomas told the state police what he knew about the 1930 lynching and the murder in Martinsville. He agreed to testify, if it ever came to that, despite the danger to himself and Lucinda.

And he released the interest he held on the church property under his grandfather's will. Attorney Shambaugh went to the circuit court for an equitable reformation of the original grant. The committee contacted the Catholic Church to see if they were still interested. And the sale of the old church and the building of the new began to move forward again.

In fact, the latter part of June, we had the groundbreaking for the new church out south of Wabash. There would be plenty of room for us to grow. The new church would have a gymnasium with a full basketball court, twice the classroom space for Sunday School, and a sanctuary four times the size of the old one.

Thomas and Lucinda were there for the ground-breaking ceremony, wielding shovels. They looked like different, happier people. Lucinda was back to teaching Sunday School. And smiling a lot. She had started hugging me again.

The next Saturday dawned bright and hot. Mom and I went out to weed peas and beans. Weeding was one of my least favorite jobs, so I was very glad when Grampa called and asked if I could come help him pick strawberries. Strawberry season only lasted a few weeks. We ate as many fresh as we wanted and then froze the rest.

Thad was helping Grampa when I got there, but eating as many as he picked. He had red juice all down his shirt. "Oh, Thad, how gross."

Karen was picking berries she would use to make strawberry jam for the fair. Following the basic *Joy of Cooking* recipe, she picked the best berries, cleaned them, and then heated to the juice stage with four cups of sugar per quart of berries. After the mixture boiled, it was allowed to cool and lemon juice was added before it went into pint jars and was sealed with hot wax.

RED RED STRAWBERRY JAM

Wash, dry well, and stem 1 quart perfect strawberries.
Place in 10-inch very heavy cooking pot cutting into a few berries to release a little juice.
Cover with 4 cups sugar, then stir the mixture over low heat until it has "juiced up". Then raise the heat to moderate and stop stirring. When the whole is a bubbling mass, set your timer for exactly fifteen minutes (seventeen, if the berries are very ripe). From this point do not disturb. You may take a wooden spoon and streak it slowly through the bottom to make sure there is no sticking. When the timer rings, tilt the pot. You should see in the liquid at the bottom a tendency to set. Slide the pot off the heat. Allow the berries to cool uncovered. Sprinkle surface with juice of half a lemon. When cool, stir the berries lightly and place in sterile jars.

Rebecca and Dick were married in the old Quaker style on a beautiful Sunday afternoon. A member of the Marriage Oversight Committee opened the service by talking briefly about Quaker weddings. Then instead of a minister presiding as in "modern" weddings, the bride and groom spoke the vows to each other. Guests were invited to speak. Everyone present was asked to sign a certificate indicating they had witnessed the marriage ceremony. It was a simple and moving occasion. At least it brought tears to my eyes, as I sat by Nate.

"In the presence of the Lord and before these Friends, I take thee, Dick, to be my husband, promising to be unto thee a loving and faithful wife as long as we both shall live." Nate squeezed my hand. How long had we known each other? A year already.

Nate's roommate Terry, the engineering student, took the photographs for the wedding. An amateur photohound who was constantly broke, he needed the money.

Amazingly, my helpers didn't trip or drop presents. Thad and Mark dutifully seated folks. They were such a model of correct behavior, I expected them to burst out at any minute, but it didn't happen.

So far so good, right? Well, there was one little screw-up, no big thing, just a minor glitch in the proceedings. Dear Thad's airfoil curiosity had finally invaded the church. At the point where the happy couple turned to the assembled group after saying their vows to each other, and Jerry began to play the recessional for them, a scrap of lightweight orange cloth, maybe nylon, about six inches square floated down from the upper loft like an inflated parachute, and to our amazement, hovered for several seconds directly over Dick's head, then settled. He reached up and took it off, with a smile and a shake of his head.

Karen and I knew what it was: one of Thad's aerodynamic tests gone awry. Turning in unison, we glared at the hapless child at the back of the church. As soon as we were safely out of the sanctuary, we descended upon him, and demanded information. "Sis, Cuz, it was a simple test of the lift generated from the exhaust of the organ pipes. How could I know the dang thing would choose this moment to wing into the sanctuary? It's been there for weeks!" Terry got a great snapshot of Dick's quizzical expression when the orange cloth settled on his head.

July 4 was my eighteenth birthday. Grams brought over a photo of my great great grandmother Selina Melvina, born on July 4, 1832, one hundred and twenty years before me. Grams asked me, "Wouldn't you like to know what she saw during the Civil War years here in Indiana? Did she help with the Underground Railroad? I've always wanted to know."

Nate came before noon. "Nate, the silo people will swing in any day. Do you want me to call you, so you can watch?"

"Sure, Mim, I'll come if I can."

We were sentimental about birthdays in our family. We had watermelon because I loved it and we made ice cream from scratch. Nate brought me a card and a simple silver necklace. He helped milk and feed calves, so I could loll around and feel pampered.

Mom had this to say, "My dear, I'm proud of your hard work with Stalwart. And pre-vet school at Purdue. Sometimes I wished I had a daughter who wanted ordinary things, but I'm over that, Mim. I'm proud of who you are." And she hugged me.

In the evening, Mom, Nate and I met the cousins, Aunt Maud, and Grams at White's Institute near Southwood High School for fireworks. The men were milking. We took fried chicken in a basket and blankets. We sometimes called White's a reform school, although it also provided a home for kids without parents. Grams sat on the Board and the Quaker church helped support it.

The next Monday morning, a silo-building crew of three men arrived in a semi tractor-trailer. They had already been to the farm where Dad had bought the silo, to tear it down and pack it into the semi-trailer in pieces.

It was 92 degrees outside. "Mom, I'll call the cousins!" I said.

"Good idea, Mim. I'll make iced tea for the men and all of us."

The cousins and everyone came from the other farm to watch. When they pulled in, Karen and Thad joined me under the shade of the big oak, south of the barnlot. Nate was in class and I couldn't reach him.

The silo crew was Tiny, tall and 300 pounds, Larry, a thin chain smoker, and another guy, no name given, who stayed inside the trailer and threw out the pieces of the silo. We'd poured a concrete footer weeks before to provide a firm foundation for the tons of brick tile. Tiny and Larry carried the first row of tiles to the site and laid them within reach. Then they set the first tile in its footing and attached the tie-off cables. They did this again and again, clear around the footer circle. The second row of tiles mounted into grooves on the top of the first row and overlapped tile-to-tile for strength.

Tiny worked on top of the rising structure, with Larry on the ground, sending up tiles by hand or hand wench. "Can you believe he can balance up there, Mim?" Thad was mesmerized by the bulk of Tiny, walking easily around the rim.

"I know, it can't be three inches wide." We could not believe a person of his bulk could balance so easily, right before our eyes. He was entertaining as a circus act. Never a slip at a hundred feet up. The men slept in their tractor-trailer that night and took their meals with us. They ate amazing quantities. The next morning, they finished it.

Nate didn't make it in time to see the silo raising. At the end of July, he became insistent that I come to Amboy for a weekend to visit his family. Of course, I had met his father and mother, Frank and Hilda, at the Christmas program. The Daniels lived in a rambling old white frame house with wonderful Victorian curlicues on the front. They needed every room in the house, because Nate had three younger brothers. And the boys owned a Saint Bernard. When I first arrived, they were on their good behavior. Within half an hour, the place sounded like a school playground on the first sunny morning in spring. Very impressive decibel levels.

The oldest of the brothers, Don, asked me at supper if I was Nate's girlfriend. Nate handled that one with a yes. Mark, the talker of the group, was a chubby, freckled red-headed ten-year-old. He wanted to know when they could visit the farm and drive the tractor. Six-year-old Tim chimed in, "I wanna play in the haymow!" I looked at Nate. "Been telling some stories, I see."

"Yep, but only true ones. About that two-foot long rat we saw in the corn bin and the hundred-foot stack of bales in the barn."

After supper, Mrs. Daniels insisted I use my time to be with Nate, not washing dishes (a woman after my heart), so we walked around Amboy, a nice little town with a pretty red brick Quaker church. Our destination was really his dad's veterinary clinic, which I was dying to see. The Daniels' small animal practice catered to the town and the surrounding countryside. The building was concrete-block, not pretty but solid. The tables and counters were stainless steel, and they gleamed.

"We have a cleaning service that comes in daily to disinfect." There was a surgery, several treatment rooms where intake and routine treatment were done, and a grooming room with a large tub, supplies and equipment hanging on the wall. And of course, the kennels for animals that must stay overnight. The dogs in the kennel started barking the moment we opened the front door of the clinic. Two dogs, a cat, and a hamster were in for the night.

"I don't know what kind of practice I'm after, Nate. I can see this is a really good set-up for your dad and the community. But something tells me I would miss the work of a large animal practice. That's where I'm headed at this point. Back to the farm." One of the things I loved about Nate was that he didn't try to tell me what I wanted to do.

Chapter Seventeen

County Fair started the next weekend. I knew I had to start work on Dad and fast, if I was to have any hope of bringing Stalwart home to sire Holstein calves. "Dad, I know we've got Stalwart entered in the beef division because of his size. But if he doesn't win, could we consider keeping him on the farm as our Holstein bull? We wouldn't have to buy him, so there's no acquisition cost. I know he's big, but we now own the Angus to bring birth size down. We need to reinforce the Holstein quality of the milk when future calves are born. And if he were the father he could do that."

"I'll think about it, Mim. It never occurred to me that you'd rather have him here than win state. I need to study the herd's genealogy to see if he's too closely related to be useful. I guess it's a good thing we didn't geld him, if that's the way you feel." It had taken a lot of argument to convince Dad not to geld Stalwart, but something had told me, even a year ago, not to.

"Mim, I'll go this far—I'll check the lineage of Rosebud's dam to see how the cows in the herd are connected genetically. Since Stalwart's sire came in an artificial insemination tube, we already know for a fact those are new genes."

"Thanks, Dad."

Even with this opening from Dad, I didn't see a way clear to taking Stalwart out of the competition. He had been bred and groomed for the fair. How could I deprive him (and me) of the opportunity to see how he measured up?

And so I hoped, perversely, as fair time approached, that somehow Stalwart, my huge and gentle friend who almost died coming out backwards, would not win. Did I claim earlier to be objective about farm animals? Well, it depended. You see, the State Fair Grand Champion and Reserve Champion were auctioned right there at the fair for beef. It was a great way to get a good price. But I had finally concluded that I didn't want Stalwart to end up at some corporate barbecue. He belonged with us. Yes, I could have refused to allow him to be sold, even if he won Grand Champion. But it would have been embarrassing for 4-H.

Anyhow, County Fair time arrived. Our Wabash County fairgrounds were fairly small, but we had a good-sized midway for the kids and youth, and the 4-H barns and buildings were well-maintained. I drove Dad's truck hauling the trailer for Stalwart and Thad's hog. Thad and Karen rode with me, arguing all the way, because Thad wanted to sit by the window in the truck. I was glad to arrive. Siblings.

After we delivered Stalwart safely to his stall, I forked in clean straw, and then we took Thad's hog over to the swine barn. Karen went on over to the 4-H building to set up her strawberry jam entry, while I got Stalwart's water, hay and grain. Afterwards, Thad and I swung by on foot to pick Karen up.

We hit the midway for rides and food. It wasn't five minutes before Thad saw friends from school and cut away to hang with them. "Dad said we have to be in the barn by ten," Karen called after him.

"Yeah, yeah, I'll beat you back," he called to us. We two rode the calmer rides, the Ferris Wheel and the Scrambler. I ate a Lemon Shake-up and a hot dog. Karen had cotton candy. We watched our basketball coach get dunked for charity. Then we went to Stalwart's stall and groomed him, a major job now. He nuzzled my arm. What a sweetheart.

After we checked hay and water, I set up the cots in front of the stall, while Karen went over to the hog barn to check on Thad. Sure enough he had his cot up, and he and his buddies were telling stories. Our barn was beginning to quiet down by eleven. Before we dozed off, I told Cousin Karen about wanting Stalwart to come home from State Fair. "You'd give up winning so Stalwart could come home? You could use the money from the auction for school."

"This is weird. I'm usually so rational. But I can replace money. Can't replace Stalwart."

Morning and Thad arrived too soon. The sun was already August hot as we headed for the Friends Church food booth where we ate a breakfast of fried eggs, bacon, toast and grape jelly. Karen and I drank coffee and Thad had orange juice. Each of us would be back there later to work a shift.

Judging started at ten o'clock in the cattle category. I had to have Stalwart fed, watered, combed and in line by then. I raced back from breakfast and grabbed his comb. Mom and Dad pulled up in the blue Fairlane and offered help. I turned over half the currying to Dad, one side for each of us. Mom refilled Stalwart's water trough and hay rack. On the dot of ten, I had him in line at the entryway to the small arena where judging took place.

It wasn't easy getting him there. He didn't like confusion, people and other animals. My control over him didn't extend far. Emotionally he cared about me because I'd always taken care of him. The heavy ring in his nose provided psychological control. Even though Stalwart could have thrown me over his shoulder with a toss of his head, he wouldn't have wanted to hurt his nose. And he knew it would hurt because he had pulled against it before. A nose ring was like a pierced earring. You wouldn't give someone a chance to yank on it on purpose.

Anyhow, his competitors were already in the arena. I led Stalwart to the center of the sawdust circle and got him set up beside the others. The judges began to work their way animal to animal, filling in points on forms. The eventual placing was based both on the judge's rating on standard measures and the relative ranking compared to the other entries. As I watched the judges work their way around the arena, I compared Stalwart to the others I could see.

Thad and I had been practicing cattle judging together for years, since I had my first calf, a heifer. We'd evaluated Stalwart critically since the day he was born. Height, weight, depth of chest. Bulls and steers should be deep-chested. Stalwart won in all categories that I could see.

Blue ribbon time at the Fair.

If I hadn't been there the night he was born, I'd probably have been more impressed.

To make a long story short, he did win. All the while that excited relatives and friends, including Thomas and Lucinda, congratulated us and flashcubes were going off, a picture of Stalwart in our meadows was running through the back of my mind. Fathering beautiful Holstein calves, not in some home freezer in little hamburger patties. On a more positive note, Karen won Best of Show for her strawberry jam. She also would go to state representing Wabash County.

Thad's purebred Chester white earned him a red ribbon. Although he could have chosen to take his hog on to State Fair even without a blue, Thad sold him in the auction at the end of the fair. The County Extension Agent organized the auction and the kids made good money, double or triple the market price. We cheered Thad and his hog wildly from the stands, as he got fifty cents a pound. Karen and I had our pictures in the *Wabash Plain Dealer* the next day, with her jam and Stalwart.

Chapter Eighteen

State Fair followed quickly on the heels of Indiana's county fairs. The Indianapolis fairgrounds was bounded by Fall Creek Parkway on the east and 38th Street on the south, with the grounds of the Indiana School for the Deaf on the north and a residential neighborhood on the west. The fair was quite a show. However, the first challenge was parking.

Mom and I had Stalwart in the trailer, hooked to the back of the pickup truck. His grain and several coolers were packed in the truck bed itself. Grampa, Grams, Karen and Thad were comfortable in Grampa's 1960 Olds 98, dark green, with felt interior, air conditioning, and electric windows. The Olds had a huge trunk, so the luggage and cots for all six of us fit there.

We knew our way to the cattle barn already, so Grampa headed north to park by the Deaf School. From there, they would begin hauling everything in. The guards at the main gate off 38th Street let Mom and me pull the truck and trailer close to the south end of the cattle barn to unload the bull. I parked it without a problem and got out our papers to prove Stalwart had been blood tested within forty-eight hours. The vet student on duty for the state vet's office inspected the papers and waved us on through.

I went to Stalwart's head to back him out of the trailer. Backing a bull was a trick in itself. We had been practicing it for months at home, up and down the ramps. Stalwart was irritable from all the noise and people he could hear behind him. He resisted the lead, turning his head and peering down the ramp.

When I finally got him down, I led him slowly into the barn, with

Mom scouting ahead to find my stall assignment. Stalwart was distracted, swinging his huge black and white head from side to side, looking, as I tried to lead him behind Mom. Once we got there, Mom held his lead rope while I forked straw around the stall. Then I closed him in his pen. Mom and I unloaded the truck and carried things in. Mom stayed to arrange our area while I parked the truck in the north lot. Not seeing Grampa and the others in the big parking lot, I ran back so I could help Mom, thereby getting my first whiffs of the food booths as I ran past.

Each stall had an extra space next to it that was used for tackle, feed and grooming supplies. Many families came as we did, bringing cots and card tables, essentially camping out in the stall barn.

While we were working, Grampa and Thad came into sight down the aisle, lugging a cooler between them. Grams and Cousin Karen were also visible, silhouetted against the sunlight at the north end of the barn. "How are you coming, Grampa?" I called out.

"We got it all, Mim," he yelled back.

They were smiling as they came up, even though they were lugging heavy bags and boxes of food. We loved being at the Fair so much the work didn't matter. Other people felt the same way, coming back year after year.

An hour later we had Stalwart fed and watered for the night. Mom, Grampa and Grams were setting up the card table and folding chairs, and making sounds like they would sit for a while. We cousins eyed each other, the tempting sounds and smells from outside the barn calling us.

"Uh, we're off to see the fair, Mom."

"Okay. But keep an eye out for each other," Mom called after us. We three had been here before, and we knew exactly where we were headed: the food and rides of the Midway.

Lots more dangerous-looking and nausea-producing rides than those at the Wabash County Fair were here. Much more diverse food: gyros from Greece, Chinese stir fry, southern pork barbecue, English fish and chips with malt vinegar, Italian spaghetti and meatballs. Plus standard fare like corn on the cob, chili dogs, tenderloins, hamburgers, steak sandwiches, French fries, ice cream, cotton candy, peanut butter and chocolate fudge. Urp!

The carnie booths were more sophisticated than at Wabash, but none of us was really into games of skill or chance. We liked rides. Rides that hung you upside down. Rides that jammed you into your seat and each other. Rides that plunged you into alternating light and dark, and maybe threw water in your face or blasted your ears with sound.

And so we went. By eleven, I was stuffed and tired from the constant noise and motion. I gathered up Karen and Thad, and we dragged back to the barn. Grams and Grampa were already in their cots asleep. The lights were lowered in the barn, although a few late arrivals were straggling in with their flashlights.

Mom was sitting at our table, reading by her battery-powered light. She looked glad to see us, so we sat and told her every ride we'd been on, every food we'd sampled. She and Grams and Grampa had eaten out of the coolers: cheese and crackers, grapes and cut-up vegetables. And angelfood cake Mom had brought, which Thad obligingly finished for her.

Karen and I went to the girls' restroom and washed up for the night. Thad was already asleep on his cot, wiped out. It was amazing that we could adjust to sleeping in a barn with two or three hundred other people and their livestock. But the body needed sleep, so sleep we did.

The next morning, eating breakfast at the 4-H booth, we talked about the schedules. Karen's jam was scheduled to be judged this afternoon at one o'clock in the 4-H Exhibit building, close to the northwest gate. Tomorrow, Thursday morning, would be the preliminary judging for Stalwart. If he scored high enough, he would advance to Friday night's championship round.

This meant that today and tomorrow afternoon were my major free times at the fair. "Mom, let's do the Home & Family Arts Building today, okay?"

"Yes, do you need to check on Stalwart before we go? Oh, and I need to stop by the pay phones and check in at home."

We four women headed for the adult 4-H building to spend the morning among the very best of Hoosier 4-H arts and crafts. My favorite as always was the quilt displays where I stood each year and admired the tiny stitchwork. I promised myself again that some day I would make a quilt of my own.

On the way there, Mom and I veered off to the public phones, where Mom checked in with Aunt Maud, who was cooking for the men while we were gone. Aunt Maud sent love and good wishes for success to Karen and me. Grams and Cousin Karen had gone on to the 4-H building and were watching the morning style show when we got there.

As Thad told me later, he and Grampa toured the dairy barn, checking out Stalwart's competition. I think Thad cared more about Stalwart's winning than I did. He wanted to anticipate which bulls were a threat to Stalwart's grand championship. He didn't know I no longer wanted Stalwart to win. I just wanted to relax and have a good time. Soon enough I would be studying intensely at Purdue, hopefully with Stalwart at home in our pastures.

After lunch we rallied at the 4-H Exhibit Building where the judging had already started. The huge room was crowded with entrants' families. The judges finally reached the jams, where they moved from one to the other, tasting. When they tasted Karen's, I noticed they quickly looked at each other, then went on.

"Did you see that, Karen?" I whispered. Thad turned around from in front of us and yelled, "They like it, Sis!" We shushed him.

After they tasted all of the best of the County Fair jams, the judges came back to Karen's and tasted it again. They conferred, then they attached the Grand Champion blue to her little jar. Thad started jumping up and down. The rest of us applauded.

We were thrilled! Grampa stuck his chest out and smiled broadly, which was not an everyday occurrence. To think his strawberry patch produced those superior berries! And his granddaughter made them into the state's best jam! My, my, what a good feeling.

Karen was very pleased. People around us turned to her, congratulating. Then a strange expression came over her face. She looked at her hands. Empty. She checked her shoulder. Empty. She turned frantically to Mom and Grams and me. "Have you seen my purse?"

No one had seen it. As one, we turned toward the door. Karen streaked ahead, calling out to us following her, "I must have left it at lunch." We had eaten at the Pork Producers booth over by the Cattle Barn.

The six of us made a beeline for Pork Producers. On the way, we passed the racetrack and grandstand where a harness race was in progress, the Midway, the west end of the food booths, and the Purdue Agriculture Horticulture Building. Finally we reached Pork Producers' large food booth. Karen headed for the busy counter, while I began to scan the tables.

A nice-looking young African-American, maybe sixteen years old, was sitting at the table where we had sat for lunch. In front of him, in plain view, was Karen's purse. "Karen, come here," I called out.

Leaving the counter, Karen came toward me, following my glance. She headed straight for the young man, sticking out her hand. "I'm Karen Hanley. That's my purse you've got there. I can't thank you enough for keeping it safe."

At first, he had not spotted us, being occupied eating, until he heard Karen's voice speaking to him, then he hopped up, smiling, and shook her hand. "My name is Jonathon. I was in line," he gestured toward the food line at the counter, "when you left in such a hurry. I spotted your purse after you left, so I sat down beside it and waited. No one bothered it." She pulled out a chair and sat. The rest of us gathered behind her.

Thad plunked himself down. "We were on the way to watch Sis win the Grand Championship of strawberry jam." He volunteered, "You should have seen her face when she realized she didn't have her purse!"

"I'm her cousin, Mim," I broke in, reaching across the table to shake Jonathon's hand. "Pleased to meet you, Jonathon."

Karen had her purse in her hands and was catching up with herself. She introduced Grams, Grampa and Mom. "Jonathon, you seem at home here." Grams is astute about people, body language, how people fit into their surroundings. She was right; he was relaxed as though he belonged here, not like us—we were excited in this new environment.

Jonathon smiled. "Thanks for noticing, Mrs. Hanley. I've been around fairs most of my life. It's a second home to me."

At this point, I excused myself and left them all there to make acquaintance, while I scooted on into the dairy barn to check on Stalwart. We hadn't left him alone for so long before. The big Holstein had drawn several admirers, but he was snoozing away, unconcerned. Watching the watchers, I began to worry again that I had a grand champion in my stall.

Well, nothing for it but to do our best and hope for the worst. We were due in the ring at nine the following morning for the preliminary judging. I pulled up a folding chair and sat with my head on Stalwart's flank.

"I want you to understand, I'm prouder of you than any other animal I've ever raised. You're big and beautiful and gentle, just like a bull should be. But I believe you'll be far happier as a sire of Holstein calves back home than as Grand Champion in a thousand Hoosier stomachs. Please try not to look so gorgeous tomorrow." He didn't seem to be listening.

I was certain he hadn't listened as we swept faultlessly through the Thursday preliminaries. Stalwart was groomed to a "T" ("T-bone"), and he positively strutted into that arena. I didn't lead him. He led me. Somehow he had adjusted to all the noise and people. We passed through to Friday's finals, a blue ribbon already attached to his halter.

On the way back to the stall, amidst the congratulations, I glumly nodded to Karen who fell into step alongside us. "Cuz, I need your support with this stubborn bull. He isn't listening to me. If he wins tomorrow night, he will not be going home with us. Come and talk some sense into this fool's head."

"Mim, I'll try, but I think you have to work on Stalwart's pride. I've never seen a situation where the saying, 'Pride goeth before a fall' fits any better. We have to convince him that seventy adoring cows and a cushy barn are better than a moment's glory in the center ring. Otherwise, he's gonna be barbecue." I groaned.

Unfortunately, Thad came dancing up in his overcharged way and overheard this last pithy piece of advice for the beefy one. "Mim, Sis, I'm shocked. You can't be asking this fine piece of bullhood to throw this fight? I know it's hard to say good-bye to him. Hey, I was there when he was born, too. But we have to be strong. If he's the best, he's gone."

I nodded, resignedly. Out of the mouths of babes.

Chapter Nineteen

It was on this ambivalent note that finals day dawned. Judging was late in the day, when the Friday night crowds had gathered. I patted Stalwart on the shoulder and left him to his bovine thoughts. Karen and I were off to visit Jonathon at his temporary home in one of the harness racing barns on the east end of the fairgrounds. His horse had a stall there. Jonathon was a jockey for a harness racing team.

The harness racing barns were some of the oldest structures on the fairgrounds. You could fairly smell the history. The sawdust shimmered in the sunlight filtering down from the gaps in the roof. These were not year-round buildings. Jonathon was calmly polishing tackle, but looked up and smiled when he saw us coming. "You're never going to get rid of us, Jonathon. We want to watch you drive today. When is it?"

"Okay, okay. There's a heat at eleven this morning and a final at one, if I win the heat."

"What are your colors? How will we know your rig?"

"Are you kidding? I'll be the only black human on the track." We laughed together a little sadly. Karen and I may be from rural Indiana, but we know that story.

Jonathon showed us his sulky, a lightweight aluminum frame with riding wheels. The pride he took in it was evident in the shine. And he introduced us to Peaches, his chestnut gelding, a beautifully proportioned horse.

Karen and I bought tickets for the grandstand at the ticket office up under the stands and went in early to watch a few heats. Maybe we'd learn something. Jonathon was right. We had no problem recognizing him when his heat came up. But it was because he was the best! Peaches won the heat, going away.

We cheered for them, then walked back over to the barn and found Jonathon cooling down the sweating Peaches in the space between two barns. "How did you get into this work?" I asked.

"My uncle has a business repairing tackle for the harness industry. The State Fairgrounds is only one of the harness tracks in Indiana. He gets a lot of his business from the tracks, old customers and new. I've been coming with him all my life."

"But this is seasonal, isn't it? What do you do off-season?"

"Well, it's not as seasonal as you'd think. Indiana has several tracks, and the Midwest Circuit races six months a year. The rest of the time, I work with my uncle in the repair shop."

We dragged him out for a lunch of fries and steak sandwiches at the 4-H booth before his final at one. After we ate, I split to check on Rosebud's son. He was fine, snoozing, but Mom was sitting alone, so I brought her with me to the grandstand where we found Karen, Grams and Grampa. Before the race started, I scanned the crowd, searching for familiar faces. Lots of Wabash people came to the fair.

"Hey, Mom, do you see Doc Tucker up to our right? See?" Not surprising to see him here. He was one of the vets who provided coverage for the fair itself.

Peaches was far and away the fastest trotter on the track that day. After they won the race, Mom and I climbed up to say "Hey" to the vet.

"Cecilia, where's Jim? You look downright lonely," he said to Mom.

"Where do you think he is, Doc? Home milking the cows."

"I don't care, he's got to come down here. Mim's bull is in the ring tonight, isn't he? I stopped off at the barn, and I swear that boy is looking awfully good." My heart sank. Doc knows cattle.

We swung by the harness barn to congratulate Jonathon. I left the mob visiting with him, while I went back to groom Stalwart for this evening's festivities. "Never let it be said that we didn't look good in our final days, huh, boy? No grill too good for you?"

Grams and Grampa wandered in, hand-in-hand, and told me about their day. Seems they attended a program for prospective buyers of Air Stream travel trailers. You know, the silver cigar of the road. And they were enamored of the idea of getting one.

I was shocked, let me tell you. Rooted in the farm all of their lives, my grandparents were supposed to stand still. How could a life on the road appeal to them now?

"Mim, it's just your idea of us that's threatened here, not our love for the farm or you. This is only a thought, dear. We've been in one place our entire lives. We want to see the country. Besides, there are plenty of Quaker outreach projects we'd like to visit." Yeah, I felt better already. I was going to have to work on myself about this one.

I wasn't hungry for supper. Too much all coming together at once. Before I knew it, Stalwart and I were entering the arena, and people were applauding. I breathed a prayer that God would have His way, then looked up in the stands and found my row of supporters: Mom, Karen, Jonathon, Grams and Grampa. No Thad. Come to think of it, I hadn't seen him in hours. Where the heck was the kid? He was so all-fired wrapped up in Stalwart's winning.

From that point, I got busy in the ring, lining up Stalwart with the others in the center. Next time I looked up, Dad and Nate had appeared, sitting next to Mom. My smile widened by two inches. I stood up straighter. And, feeling my change of attitude, so did Stalwart. Uh-oh, it didn't pay to look too good!

The three judges, with the usual clipboards, worked their way down the row. Each animal took about two minutes, as they walked around him, inspecting. One of them was a short guy, maybe 5'3," wearing a complete western outfit, polished boots, western-style shirt, jeans and chaps, and cowboy hat. A real dude of a judge. As they approached us, I amused myself by wondering how much he paid for that get-up. Would these be the people who sent my Stalwart to Hamburger Palace? I prayed for third place.

Just when the three judges got themselves spread out around Stalwart, at that precise moment, sirens began to shriek, it sounded like

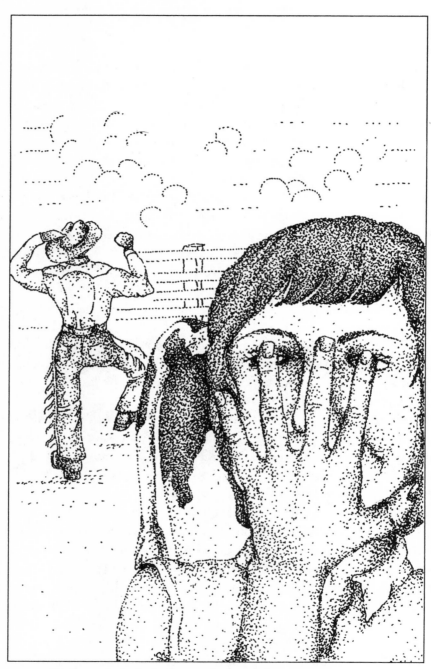

Stalwart's dude judge and the unfortunate accident.

right outside the building. And I didn't mean one siren. I meant ten. The crowd, smelling smoke, leaped to their feet, and began milling. The adrenaline was palpable.

Stalwart jerked against the lead from his nose ring. And then his perfectly predictable reaction to this additional stress was to deposit a fresh, steaming load of bull poop, directly on the shiny new boots of the dude judge. A cow patty so big I heard the "ploop" through the noise. Direct hit.

"Congratulations, Stalwart," I crooned into his massive face. "I think you've done it." My eyes sought out the face of the little judge. He was swearing, jumping up and down and thwhacking his foot on the ground sideways. Put on quite a show, he did. All the while the sirens were wailing at ear-splitting levels. Lucky for the judge they were making so much noise.

Thank heaven for human nature! Two other superior pieces of beef won the grand and reserve champion ribbons and would be auctioned off as soon as the pandemonium died down.

The little judge wiped his boots with his bandanna and shot dirty looks our way. Turned out he was the auctioneer, too. He started his chant from up in the announcers' booth, trying not to lose the crowd to the fire. "Hey, bidder, bidder . . . ." As he started in, the sirens screamed louder. Surely there was a major fire, sounded like it was coming from the east end of the fairgrounds.

Things disintegrated fast. As I dragged Stalwart toward the south exit of the arena, in the direction of the cattle barn, I saw Jonathon running out the east door toward Peaches and the harness barn. Nate reached me just as I cleared the doorway from arena to hallway. Mom and Dad were right behind him. Nate had to talk right in my ear: "Your dad told me that you didn't want him to win. Good thinking, Mim. We need him back on the farm."

I was glad he agreed with me, but what really mattered at that moment was the "we" in that sentence. Despite the fact that I had two thousand pounds of thrust on my arm, I turned my head and kissed him quick.

I still had to shout to be heard, as we cleared the outer door on the south toward the stall barn. "Nate, something's wrong, I can feel it. Thad's been gone since morning, and that fire is right where Jonathon's Peaches is stabled."

"Wait, who's Jonathon?"

Dad and Mom were pulling even with us by then. "Dad," I yelled above the crowd and the sirens, "We've got to go look for Thad! Can you take Stalwart back to his stall and stay with him?"

"Sure." Dad took the lead from my hand and quickly moved in close by Stalwart's head, smoothly distracting him from my movement away. "But you keep us posted." Off we moved toward the crackling and the smoke.

Before us, around the circle drive that ringed the fairgrounds, the flames were yellow and red in the direction of the old harness barns. Whether it was Jonathon's I couldn't be sure from there, but whichever one it was, it looked hopeless. The hoses were pouring water into the shell of the burning barn and onto the barns next to it. "It might be Jonathon's barn," I told Nate, as we headed that way, slowed by the crowds ahead of us.

"But who's Jonathon?"

"Oh, he's the guy who saved Karen's purse from being stolen this morning." For some reason, Nate still looked confused.

We passed the empty clogging stage from which music blared. Everyone was over watching the fire. By this point, we were moving through crowds of onlookers who had gotten there before we could unload Stalwart. We picked our way to the front of the crowd, held back by the police line around the burning barn. Sparks were floating skyward. It would be a close thing to protect the barns nearby, which were also tinder boxes.

"Nate, see the black kid in police custody over there? That's Jonathon." Now I was really irritated, as what I saw was seeping into my muddled brain. Jonathon in handcuffs? What, the police thought he had set the fire? There was no way he could have had anything to do with that barn on fire, especially with Peaches and his sulky inside.

Jonathon, policeman, crowd and burning building.

Besides, he'd been with my family the entire day from his first heat this morning on. We were his alibi, for heaven's sake. "We have to get over there and make those cops listen."

I pulled Nate up to the police barrier, and we worked our way around to a point closer to Jonathon, who was standing with his back to the crowd. "I know him—I can vouch for where he's been." I leaned in toward the cop who was holding the barricade closed. A black cop. He looked to where I was pointing at Jonathon, nodded and let me through. Sometimes I know what to do.

As we hurried across the grass between the crowd and Jonathon, the light and heat from the burning barn flared, showering us with sparks. The crowd groaned behind us, the people at the front jumping back, knocking down those behind them. The cop who was holding Jonathon's handcuffed arm saw us approaching, and so did Jonathon. A small smile started in the corner of his mouth. "Mim! Thank God!" Beyond me, across the circle, he spotted Karen, Grams and Grampa also picking their way through the barricade. His smile widened.

"Officer, this man has been with us," I gestured back at Jonathon, "since before one this afternoon. Why do you have him under arrest? What, was he the only black man around the harness barn?" Jonathon shot a frightened look at me. I guess I was screwing up. In contrast, Jonathon knew cops: he was born and raised in Indianapolis. He knew how not to talk to them. Karen reached us and did an amazingly quick survey of our faces, from me around to the cop. She swung in smoothly between his reddening face and mine.

"Officer, Jonathon has been with one or all of us from early afternoon uninterrupted right through to now. We can vouch for his whereabouts. Besides, do you realize his horse was inside that barn?" She was just in time. Right then I got distracted by Thad's frightened, dirty face, peering out at me from the crowd. He was gesturing to me madly, waving me over. Nate was watching, and he nodded me toward Thad, as he turned away to talk to Jonathon.

I broke away from the group around Jonathon, and ran to Thad, behind the barricade. He was scratched up, panting heavily and constantly scanning the people around us. I grabbed his arm. He was sweating and shaking.

"Where in the world have you been? What's going on?"

"Mim, you've got to help me. I saw the guys who started this fire. They set it with gasoline. Then they saw me and they chased me clear around the fairgrounds, through the Midway, the booths, the barns. They've got weapons, Mim. Knives, guns. They'll find me here, if we don't get moving." His survival instinct was on full.

"No, no, Thad, we can't fight them alone. We've got to get you to the police." I had come full circle on trusting the police. Who could explain? All I knew was, no Indianapolis hood was gonna hurt my cousin.

I pulled him out of the crowd and to the cop holding Jonathon, still in handcuffs. Thad was scared to death, shaking. I could tell it was for real. He kept scanning for the hoods. Hey, we were from cow country, okay? We weren't used to guys chasing us with knives. He told the cop the same story, with more detail about what he'd seen and where he'd run.

I let Karen get in between me and the cop, so I didn't screw up this time. The cop seemed to feel bad about arresting Jonathon just for a minute. He explained while unlocking the cuffs, "Some guy told me he'd seen Jonathon hanging around the barn, so I thought I'd better hold him."

Meanwhile, Jonathon's barn had burned to the ground. The cop took Thad to report to the officer in charge at the fire, then to look for the three guys. Maybe they were still on grounds, looking for Thad. Dumber things have happened.

Jonathon rubbed his wrists. He and Karen were talking about finding Peaches. I had just realized Nate was gone, when he came walking around the far end of the next barn, leading Peaches and a slim, middle-aged black man. Jonathon's uncle. Introductions and reunions occurred. Then the others took Peaches to find a stall for her to stay the night.

I pulled Nate over to lean against a police car, while I caught him up on the events of this day, starting with the jam competition and Karen's purse. "So how did you find Peaches? How could you know what she even looks like?"

"Well, while you went to talk sense into Thad, I asked Jonathon where his horse was. He didn't get a chance to run into the burning barn when he got here from the cattle judging, before he got busted by the over-eager cop. Of course he was really upset, not knowing if she was burning up or being stolen. I figured I could just mosey around a little while and get things straightened out. When I got beyond the next barn north, I found a chestnut that matched the description, being held by an older guy who looked an awful lot like Jonathon. He had Peaches pretty well calmed down. It had to be the uncle. I just walked up, identified myself and said I could take him to Jonathon. Sure enough, it was his uncle."

"You're so resourceful."

He pulled me close, me in my manure boots, smelling of smoke. "What a life I lead when I'm with you! From learning to drive a tractor to losing a grand championship and saving a friend! Never a dull moment."

I was in heaven.

Chapter Twenty

Things calmed down considerably in the aftermath of the fair. Stalwart was home again, with his State Fair blue ribbon tacked above his stall in the red barn. Soon he would be siring calves with the part-Angus heifers, to avoid the large calf problem. Dad would carefully monitor bloodlines. We would see how it went.

The police caught the three hoodlums who set the fire. Thad identified them from the mug books, when he went downtown to make a formal statement. He had several close-up looks at each of them at the fairgrounds and another from behind a one-way screen at a line-up the next morning. Pretty nifty police work to pick them up so fast. Me, I kept out of the way, and let Cousin Karen handle the family's connection with the police. I could see now how well-matched she was to her career plans.

Thad was still a little pale under his freckles that next day. He told us the story in great detail. He was on the way back to meet the family at the arena for Stalwart's judging, after hanging out with Wabash County friends most of the day. The adults made it clear at this point in the narrative that he should have let someone know who he was with.

Anyhow, around seven, he swung behind the harness barns on his way back, just to see what was back there. And he saw three young men pouring gasoline on a straw pile, then throwing a match on it. It roared up right away, setting the barn ablaze in seconds.

Unfortunately, they saw him, too, and began chasing him. I guess they went counterclockwise clear around the grounds, dodging and grabbing, before he eluded them in the cattle barn. During the chase, Thad knocked popcorn out of a fairgoer's hands, then the chasers ran right over the guy. Little kids were screaming. A couple of carnies tried to stop Thad until they saw the three coming after him. They let Thad go and slowed down the pursuers. When he got into the cattle barn, he hid behind a big bull with a grand champion ribbon on his halter who was nowhere near as good-looking as Stalwart.

The police did find out why the barn was burned. One of the culprits was angry because a horse sale had fallen through. One of the horses was in that barn, and his owner would be out thousands of dollars.

Jonathon and Karen were corresponding. She was encouraging him to finish his high school diploma by GED and then pick up a few college courses in the off-season. We would visit him when we travelled downstate for the trial.

Karen, Thad and I were talking in the haymow the next weekend. Old habits die hard. The haymow was half-filled again with hay from our fields, as winter would be coming again soon.

"Mim, I'm happy Stalwart didn't win. I like having a bull at each farm. And after all, I was there the day he was born," said my cousin Thad.

"I'm glad you're glad, Thad."

Cousin Karen was thinking about weightier things. "The police assumed Jonathon was guilty because he was the only black man in sight, you know it's true."

"If I hadn't come back there and told them who started it, they would have arrested him, wouldn't they?" Thad was still putting it all together.

I chipped in my two cents' worth, as Grandfather Gurtner would say. "Yes, and doesn't it make you wonder how far we've really come since 1925?"